"Stay."

Britt sounded insistent.

"Not a good idea—" Coop began, but she cut him off.

"With me."

"Britt..."

"I don't want to sleep alone... Dang it! I've reported the death toll and that number's going to rise before this storm goes away. People have lost everything. People have died. There's so much bad out there tonight. Is it wrong that I want something good? To feel strong arms around me? To be kissed?" Her voice trailed off. "I'm...scared, okay?"

"I'm scared too, Britt."

"I just want to feel something...real. Something life affirming. Something with *you*."

* * *

Twice the Temptation by Silver James is part of the Red Dirt Royalty series.

Dear Reader,

Oklahoma has been Tornado Alley since before I was born and, since I'm older than red dirt, that's a very long time. Our local TV stations are on the leading edge of weather technology due to the number and severity of storms. The National Weather Service even got in on the act when they located their Severe Storms Lab down in Norman, Oklahoma, next to the University of Oklahoma's School of Meteorology.

I've lived through some of the big storms, including the two F5 tornadoes that hit central Oklahoma on May 3, 1999, and May 20, 2013. The University of Oklahoma storm chase team's mobile Doppler radar recorded wind speeds of over 300 miles per hour during the 1999 storm, setting a record. At 2.6 miles, the El Reno tornado on May 31, 2013, is the widest tornado on record. Four storm chasers lost their lives in that one.

As a member of a search-and-rescue team, I reported with my teammates to the scene of the 1999 storm. Sooner or later, I knew I'd have to write about a storm chaser. Watching coverage of a hurricane slamming into southern Texas gave me an idea, and Britt Owens, our heroine, was born. Then I had to find the perfect hero. Cooper Tate raised his hand to volunteer. Thus, this book came to life.

I hope you enjoy Britt and Coop's story. We're coming into storm season again, so stay safe and weather aware!

Happy reading,

Silver James

SILVER JAMES

TWICE THE TEMPTATION

ISBN-13: 978-1-335-23275-5

Twice the Temptation

This edition published by arrangement with Harlequin Books S.A.

For questions and comments about the quality of this book, please contact us at CustomerService@Harlequin.com.

Harlequin Enterprises ULC
22 Adelaide St. West, 40th Floor
Toronto, Ontario M5H 4E3, Canada
www.Harlequin.com

Printed in U.S.A.

Silver James likes walks on the wild side and coffee. Okay. She *loves* coffee. Warning: her muse, Iffy, runs with scissors. A cowgirl at heart, she's also been an army officer's wife, a mom and a grandmother, and has worked in the legal field, fire service and law enforcement. Now retired from the real world, she lives in Oklahoma and spends her days writing with the assistance of her two Newfoundland rescue dogs, the cat who rules them all and the myriad characters living in her imagination. She loves interacting with readers on her blog and Facebook. Find her at silverjames.com.

Books by Silver James

Harlequin Desire

Red Dirt Royalty

Cowgirls Don't Cry
The Cowgirl's Little Secret
The Boss and His Cowgirl
Convenient Cowgirl Bride
Redeemed by the Cowgirl
Claiming the Cowgirl's Baby
The Cowboy's Christmas Proposition
Twice the Temptation

Visit her Author Profile page at Harlequin.com, or silverjames.com, for more titles.

You can also find Silver James on Facebook, along with other Harlequin Desire authors, at Facebook.com/harlequindesireauthors!

Dedicated to the weathermen I watched on TV
growing up—Jim and Gary—and to "Tornado"
Payne and his weather crew at "Oklahoma's Own,"
and to all the storm chasers in central Oklahoma.
Your efforts and expertise keep us safe,
so here's a big shout-out and thank-you!

One

Cooper Tate was a man comfortable in his own skin. He might be the chief operating officer of a billion-dollar oil and gas company, but he was far more likely to be found in jeans and a T-shirt working alongside his crews in the oil patch than in the boardroom. He left the fancy duds to his cousin, Cord Barron, the CEO of Barron Explorations. To Coop's mind, the key word in his COO title was *Operations*. If he couldn't do all that stuff out in the field, he shouldn't be the one in charge.

Now, as the winds of a Category 4 hurricane roared around him, he might have to rethink that stance. Living in Oklahoma, he was used to the wind sweeping down the plains, but this? He'd take a tornado over a hurricane any time.

The huge crew-cab he drove shuddered under the

wind's onslaught. The windshield wipers couldn't keep up with the downpour. Two more miles. He only had two more miles before reaching the Beaumont field office of BarEx. He'd be safe from the storm there. He hoped.

After what seemed like a century, but in reality was only about twenty minutes, Coop pulled into the parking lot. The building was the only one with lights, which meant the emergency generator had kicked on when the area lost power. After a series of strong hurricanes, Cord had rebuilt the field offices all along the Gulf Coast. All of them were supposed to stand up to a Category 5 hurricane. All of them had emergency generators that ran on natural gas straight from the company's own pipelines. He'd tried to convince the skeleton crew that stuck around to help him shut down the rigs to stay at the office but they'd all gone to their own homes, wanting to protect their families and property.

He caught a break in the rainbands and used it to lock up his truck and dash around the building. All the hurricane shutters were secure. The roof looked intact, and all the outbuildings appeared to be holding their own. He was as secure as he could be until Lolita decided she'd had enough of south Texas and moved on. Locking and bolting the main door, he settled in for a long, lonely wait. Yeah, he was a wuss. Storms weren't his thing. Never had been, not since he was caught out in a severe thunderstorm that turned tornadic when he was a kid.

Pushing that memory to the back of his mind, Coop checked the interior. Supplies lined the walls of the workshop, all up on stacked pallets just in case floodwaters breached the outer doors. The refrigerator hummed along nicely, and all the lights worked, along with the microwave, industrial-size coffeemaker, and the small gas range in the kitchenette adjacent to the break room. He started a pot of coffee and snagged a cold bottle of water from the fridge. Dropping onto a couch, he clicked on the big-screen TV mounted to the wall.

All the local and cable news channels were running wall-to-wall storm coverage. He considered shoving a DVD into the player or checking one of the cable movie channels but stopped when one of the reports focused on Beaumont.

"Water continues to rise—" Wind whipped the reporter's words away as he leaned into the gale. "Expecting hundreds of rescues—" The picture froze, then pixelated before the telecast returned to the in-studio hosts. "We've lost our feed..."

Hundreds of rescues? That would depend on a lot of factors. Would levees hold? Had people evacuated? He doubted many of them had. Lolita's path had wobbled and then made a hard right, heading straight for Beaumont, instead of farther down the coast around Houston. Houston had been ready, mandatory evacuations in force for days. Beaumont? Not so much. Most people were probably sheltering in place. Some might have made it to one of the approved shelters. He hoped there weren't many who'd been caught in the inevitable traffic jams headed out of town. With only one interstate, and that one running basically east and west, there weren't many ways out. Plus, a lot of the evacuees from Houston had come to Beaumont.

The wind screamed around the building, raising goose bumps on his skin. "Not a tornado," he reminded himself. Uneasy, despite his attempts to reassure himself, he paced the room, continuously clicking through channels. The electronic alert from the weather radio on a nearby table made his heart race. The computerized voice advised everyone to shelter in place, reminded them that when the eye hit, to stay put, and that the storm swell would send Lake Sabine and connecting bayous to 500-year-flood levels. Beaumont was about twenty miles from the Gulf Coast, but lakes and bayous peppered the area.

Rain beat on the roof like rolling thunder and the wind continued to howl. He grabbed a cup of coffee, hoping the caffeine would steady his nerves. Weather was so not his thing. "Not afraid," he muttered. "Just cautious. There's a difference." Except his brothers still teased him. Well, that was their problem, right? They hadn't been out on horseback that day. They hadn't had to hunker down in the caved-in root cellar of an abandoned cabin. And they hadn't lost their favorite horse during the tornado.

Morose now, he clicked through the movie channels until he found one with car chases and explosions. Cooper turned up the volume in a vain attempt to drown out the storm.

"This is Britt Owens, reporting live from Beaumont, Texas, for KOCX, Oklahoma's Original." Britt signed off from the live telecast then reached to turn off the camera. Her cameraman and chase assistant, Leo, was in the hospital, having been beaned by a flying trash can earlier that day. That the former football lineman could be leveled so easily was a shock. She'd wanted to call off the live updates but the station back in Oklahoma City had overruled her.

She broke down the camera and tripod, stuffing them into her storm chaser's truck. She hadn't planned on growing up to be an adrenaline junkie but after surviving an Oklahoma tornado as a kid, she'd set her sights on becoming a meteorologist. Her original goal had been to work in the lab with computers. Her bank account and student loans had other ideas. Which was why she was currently in this predicament.

Britt hadn't volunteered for hurricane duty. Yes, they were amazing weather phenomena, but tornadoes were what got her pulse racing. And even though hurricanes spawned tornadoes on the leading edge, she was stuck covering the eye of the storm since the station paid the bills. Secretly, she wanted to be the one naming storms, not that she held a grudge and would use the names of people she didn't get along with for inspiration.

The wind blasted around the corner, sending her slamming into the side of her truck. *Ouch.* That would leave a bruise.

The intensifying storm had jumped from a Category 3 to Category 4 in an hour and the rainbands now swept in faster and faster. Time to take shelter. As soon as she edged her truck out into the main force of the wind, the big vehicle shuddered. She glanced at the weather instruments panel. As winds currently topped out at 137 miles per hour, shelter had become a necessity. Between rain and darkness, she could barely see the road. Debris passed on both sides. The truck, set up for storm chasing, had all sorts of computronics and instruments. It was big, with shatterproof glass and run-flat tires—all important for getting her through this in one piece.

She should have stayed at the hospital after dropping off Leo. Too bad her curiosity and the urging of the senior meteorologist back home overrode her logical brain, feeding into her inner adrenaline junkie. The wheel jerked in her hands and the truck hydroplaned. She fought for control, and managed to keep the vehicle on the road, pointed in the right direction. No way would she make it to the hotel. Or the emergency operations center in the basement of city hall.

A light gleamed through the sheets of water pounding her windshield. Someone had power? Maybe it was a fire station. She headed for the light, suppressing the spasm threatening to lock her muscles. A huge black blob appeared in her peripheral vision. She slammed on the brakes; the truck fishtailed and finally stopped. Once the world quit spinning, she discovered she could still breathe, once she remembered how.

Britt was *not* going to die. Not tonight.

A steady *thump thump thump*, sounding like his heartbeat echoing in Cooper's ears, was a bass drum to the wailing wind. The sound came again. He hoped none of the shutters had come loose. Then he froze.

Was that a voice? He held his breath, listening hard after clicking mute on the TV.

Thump thump thump. "Is anybody here? Let me in!"

He set the coffee cup down so hard it sloshed and then he was sprinting for the front door. He didn't hesitate to unlock and yank off the brace bar to wrestle the door open. A woman stumbled into him, and he automatically wrapped his arms around her to steady her. He had to lean into her, fighting the wind to get the door closed and secured again. Once that was done, he discovered he'd pressed her back against the door.

He held his breath, aware that his body liked her—rain-soaked clothes and all—pressing against him. Yeah, parts of him seemed a little *too* happy about their position. He loosened his arms, but she didn't move. Her arms remained wrapped around his waist. He cleared his throat. She still didn't move.

"Ah, miss?"

She raised her head, clocking him on the chin.

"Ow!"

"Oh! Sorry!" She let go but couldn't back up due to the door behind her.

Cooper stepped away, rubbing his chin. "No problem but, darlin', I gotta ask, what the devil are you doin' out in this?"

The woman scrubbed at her face. "My job." Oddly, her statement sounded more like a question.

"Bad night for it."

"Definitely." She glanced at a reception area. "I'm… confused. You aren't trying to stay open or something, are you?"

"Nope. Temporary shelter. This place can withstand a Category 5 and has a generator. I'm hunkered down here for the duration."

She inhaled, waiting a long moment before exhaling. "Well, I'm glad you are. I wouldn't have lasted out there much longer." She stuck out her hand. "Britt Owens."

"Cooper Tate." He wrapped his hand around hers, very aware how his rough callouses scraped against the soft skin of her palm. Then he realized she was shivering. "Let me get you some dry clothes. And food. Coffee. Or hot tea. Got both."

He ushered her to the break room where he dug out a pair of sweats and a T-shirt from his duffel bag. Pointing toward the bathroom, he said, "You can change in there."

When Britt came out, Cooper pretended he didn't appreciate the way she looked in his clothes, nor did he acknowledge the buzz of possessiveness that filled him. Nope. Not at all. Something crashed outside and they both jumped, which jerked him back to reality in a heartbeat.

They ate sandwiches mostly in silence, though she explained she was in Beaumont to cover the storm for a TV station. When she yawned, Coop suggested they try to sleep. "There's an air mattress in the office down the hall. You can sleep there. I'll bunk on the couch."

Britt eyed the couch, gave him a once-over and rolled her eyes. "Yeah, like you'll fit."

"Not gonna argue, darlin'. My momma raised me to be a gentleman."

Elbow planted on the table, she leaned into her palm. Her eyes were brown, he realized as he got a good look at her. And they were flecked with a shade of gold close to the color of her hair. Her face, an almost perfect oval, was pale and drawn, dark circles marring her skin. Her full lips, even as they drooped with exhaustion, ignited an urge to kiss them. He resisted because she looked worn out. He brushed a tendril of hair off her face and whispered, "C'mon, weather girl. Let's get you to bed."

She followed him to the office he used when in town. A thick air mattress, almost the height of an actual bed, sprawled in the open space between door and desk. It even had sheets and pillows. He grabbed a pillow and turned to leave. Britt blocked the door. Coop arched a brow, confused.

"Stay." She sounded insistent.

"Not a good idea—" he began before she cut him off with a breathy, "With me."

Oh, yeah. He wanted to do that. Which made it a really bad idea. "Look, Britt..."

She fumbled with the hem of the T-shirt she wore, twisting it in her fingers before she huffed out a breath, as if she'd made up her mind. She met his gaze. "I don't want to sleep alone. Okay?"

She was adamant, despite the nervous movement of her fingers, and she sounded almost angry. Honestly? Coop didn't want to sleep alone either. Which made him feel like a big ol' wuss but those were the breaks. Curious about her reasons, he asked. "Why?"

"Why what?"

"Why do you want to sleep with me?"

She blinked at him several times before a speculative

look slid across her features. "Why not? You're a good-lookin' guy. I'm not exactly coyote ugly—"

That startled a burst of laughter from him. She was definitely not ugly. Her face suffused with color as her eyes narrowed and her lips thinned out. "Go ahead and laugh but…dang it!" She threw her hands up, beginning to pace the narrow confines of the office. "I watched my cameraman get slammed by flying debris today. He's in the hospital. He could have died. I've reported the death toll and that number is only going to rise before this witch of a storm goes away. People have lost everything. Eve…ry…thing."

She stopped right in front of him. "People have died." Her voice fell to a husky whisper, the edges still sharpened by anger. And fear. "There's so much bad out there tonight. Is it wrong that I want something good? That I want to feel strong arms around me? To be kissed? To…" Her voice trailed off, her cheeks no longer pink as reality seeped back into her.

"I'm…scared, okay?"

His hand caught the back of her neck and tugged her against him. "I'm scared too, Britt." Coop wasn't sure why he could admit that to a stranger—no, not a stranger. To her. To Britt. She rested her forehead against his chest and her arms circled his waist.

"I'm not crazy. I'm not a… I don't go pick up random men and proposition them."

"Shh. Didn't think you did."

"Just so you know." She was nothing if not persistent. Cooper smiled into her hair. Strands of the blond silk caught in his scruff as she tilted her head back to look up at him. "I just want to feel something…real. Something life-affirming."

Cooper didn't answer—not with words, anyway. He lowered his head, capturing her mouth. She tasted of grape jelly and peanut butter, and he swore that would be his favorite flavor from now on.

Britt leaned against him, her mouth and body softening. He deepened the kiss, taking her mouth with an urgency that swelled up from deep inside. Keeping one hand on her nape to guide the kiss, he skimmed the other over her back before cupping her rounded curves. He pressed her against his erection and she purred.

"Yes."

"Are you sure?"

"I want this. Want you."

That's all the permission he needed. He walked her to the bed and eased her down before joining her. He used both hands to touch her, slipping them under the T-shirt—*his* shirt—to trace her smooth skin before divesting her clothes. As his hands roamed, hers weren't idle, stripping off the shirt he wore before working on his belt and zipper. He pushed her hands away, and sat up to kick off his boots and jeans. He stretched out beside her, and her hands traced his abs before seeking out more private parts. Tentative fingers gripped him, and he sucked in air.

"Britt." He needed to slow down, keep his wits.

"Please?" Her whisper teased his skin. "I want this. You want it. We're alive. Let's celebrate."

The wind screamed around the building and the roof rattled, adding an exclamation—and urgency—to her words. The small part of his brain that could still think admitted she could be right. He caressed her breast as she squeezed him. His hips pumped into her hands.

"Britt." Her name was now a plea. As his free hand sought her core, finding her hot and wet, his conscience jabbed him. Condom. Swiftly, he rolled them over and he fumbled along the floor searching for his jeans and the wallet in his back pocket. He found it and the foil packet tucked inside. She arched against him and his body went on autopilot, reacting to her desire. She moaned, hips pumping against his groin. She was hot and ready for him. Condom on, her body open to him, he slid inside her, catching her soft gasp with a kiss.

Something crashed and the building shook. Britt's nails dug into his shoulders. "Hurry," she demanded, as if the end of the world was imminent. Maybe it was, if the racket outside was any indication.

Adrenaline demanded he take this woman hard and fast. The urgent noises she made indicated she wanted the same, but something coiled inside him, holding him back, something that turned the hunger for frenetic sex into a craving to make love. If there was no tomorrow, he wanted to go out surrounded by the sweetness that was Britt Owens.

As if attuned to his thoughts, she gentled beneath him, met his slow thrusts with a whispered, "Yes."

He touched her, exploring curves and skin, hair and mouth, all while he continued rocking into her, rousing them both to higher levels of passion until they both crested and tumbled into the exhaustion that lurked in the dark.

Cooper pulled Britt into his arms, and they drifted off to sleep, the sound of the howling wind a terrible lullaby.

Two

Coop rolled over expecting a warm body but found only cold sheets. Sitting up, he scrubbed the heels of his hands over his face, thinking hard. The eye of the storm had hit about 3:00 a.m., followed by more rain-bands. He vaguely remembered Britt getting up…when? Around dawn, maybe? He fumbled for his phone, read the digital numbers. Seven eleven. Too bad he wasn't in Vegas on the floor of Barron Crown Casino.

He pushed off the air mattress, found his feet and went in search of his guest. She was gone, but Gilbert Guidry, the senior toolpusher for BarEx's south Texas operations and Cajun to the soles of his boots, occupied a seat at the table, a cup of hot coffee in front of him.

"You lookin' for that pretty little *fille*?"

Cooper nodded.

"She let me in, told me to tell you she had to go be on television, and thanks." Gil pushed back from the table, fetched a cup of coffee and pressed it into Cooper's hands. "You look like you need some of this. Drink up."

Following orders, Coop did just that, wondering why it bothered him so much that Britt bailed on him. It wasn't like they had a relationship. Or anything. But still.

"You gonna put some clothes on, boss? The boat's on my truck and we're gonna be needed to help with the rescues."

True that.

A brutal eighteen hours later, Coop and Gil were headed back to the rescue command post set up for this part of town. Exhausted, hungry and desperately craving dry clothes, Coop was lost in his thoughts.

"Hello?"

Was that a voice? He cut the engine and let the boat drift.

"Somebody out there?" Gil called.

"Help! Over here." A husky—and vaguely familiar—female voice that held only a hint of panic called out.

As the boat floated toward the sound, Coop saw a light waving frantically. "We be comin', *cher*!" the toolpusher yelled.

Coop started the engine, easing the throttle. In the dark, they couldn't see what lay hidden beneath the murky water. He steered gingerly around a corner, hoping there wasn't a submerged street sign that would take out the propeller, and discovered an extended cab pickup with only six inches of window and roof showing above the rising water. Three women, two children, two dogs and a drenched cat huddled on top.

The woman with the flashlight—and familiar shape—shouted instructions. "My truck is in the middle of the street. To my right, there's a compact car submerged. My left should have a space clear enough to bring your boat alongside."

All traces of panic fled as Britt took charge. Coop pressed his lips together to hide his grin. She wore a yellow slicker with reflective tape and as she turned, he caught the emblem and writing on the back. His storm chaser worked for his cousin's TV station. Her wet hair was pulled back in a ponytail but long tendrils had worked free to plaster against her cheeks. He recognized the jut of her chin, the rounded cheeks and the determined set of her shoulders. He liked women with attitude and Britt had it in spades.

Britt handed her flashlight to a boy of about twelve and dropped to one knee to help guide the boat. Gil helped the children and dogs into the boat, then the women. Only the cat refused to move. While Gil handed out blankets, Coop considered the situation. He was not a cat guy but even he couldn't leave it to drown. The creature was big, black, with glowing yellow eyes, and it looked like it could take on a gator. He glared at the cat. It glared back.

"I can leave you for gator bait, or you can get in the boat," he said, challenging the cat. "Your choice."

His storm chaser snorted. "You really think talking like that to a cat is going to work?"

"You're more than welcome to reach over and grab the thing, weather girl," he shot back. "Last chance, cat." He waited a few seconds then placed his hand on the truck's roof and pushed off. Before he could react, the cat was climbing his arm like it was a tree, then scurrying down his back to settle in the space beneath his seat at the back of the boat.

"Huh," Britt said. "I'm impressed."

So was he, even more than the previous night when she'd fallen asleep in his arms.

After several live broadcasts, Britt jumped in to help with rescuing people and now had resigned herself to spending the night huddled atop her truck with the family she'd rescued. The roof didn't offer much room for humans or furry critters and it would have been miserable out there. Then she'd heard the growly putt-putt of a small outboard engine. Thank the weather gods for a hot guy who could out-attitude a cat. The cat hadn't been part of the original rescue. It swam over and climbed aboard after the wall of water washed down the street taking Britt by surprise and they'd all climbed to the roof. It had ignored the fat Corgi and the gentle Lab mix sharing the roof with it.

She didn't want to consider the thoughts a very hot and sexy Cooper put into her head. His looks hadn't changed since the last time she'd seen him, asleep on that air mattress barely covered by a rumpled sheet. He was in his mid-thirties, at least six feet tall, hair almost too long hidden beneath a baseball cap, broad shoulders and chest and those long, competent fingers on the boat's tiller—fingers that had done all sorts of delicious things to her body the previous night. Top it all off with blue eyes, high cheekbones, strong jaw and full lips that showed he laughed. A lot. She liked a man who laughed.

One of the kids started to fuss and Britt reached for the little girl reflexively. Her hand collided with a brawny arm. Cooper scooped up the child and settled her on one thigh. "Can you help me steer, darlin'?"

It was like he'd thrown a switch. The toddler snuggled in, tears and fussing over, as a shy smile wreathed her cherubic face.

"There anybody left back in that neighborhood?" The man who'd introduced himself as Gilbert when she'd let him into the offices that morning gestured behind the boat.

Britt lifted a shoulder in an I'm-not-sure gesture. "I heard a call go out on the scanner about a family of three who were trapped by the rising water. They didn't have a car. I wasn't far away and my truck is—" She glanced back over her shoulder. "My truck *was* four-wheel drive and customized to work in storm areas. I loaded up Becca, the kids and their dog. On the way out, we saw Mrs. Gonzales. I grabbed her and George—" She pointed to the Corgi. "We got about three blocks. I knew the water was rising but I still had clearance and then four feet of water rolled down the street."

"Yeah, that's when the levee got breached. Gotta say, *cher*, didn't expect to meet you again so soon."

"Have storm, will travel," she quipped. "Thanks for the rescue."

"You're welcome." It was Cooper who replied, and he sounded just a bit…miffed. Maybe she should have woken him up to say goodbye but hey…she wasn't good at those awkward morning afters, especially since she'd been the one to throw herself at the guy.

What had she been thinking? Oh, right. She hadn't been thinking at all, running strictly on adrenaline and the very real fear that she might not see another day. That was her story and she'd stick to it. No need to mention she was also a little embarrassed by her actions but wow. What a man to fall into bed with, regardless of the circumstances!

The puttering engine filled the silence, but Gilbert was all about asking questions. In the space of the short boat ride, she learned that Becca's husband was in the National Guard and he'd been activated, thinking they'd be safe. Mrs. Gonzales was a widow, living alone with her chubby Corgi for companionship, her kids spread across Texas. Britt hoped at least a couple of those adult children would come help their mother.

Now that they were almost safe, Britt itched to get to a computer so she could study the storm models and radar. This hurricane was a thousand-year storm. She'd saved her laptop from the flood, but it wasn't up to the task.

It wasn't long before they floated around a corner and the water glistened with lights. First responder vehicles, red-and-blue LED lights flickering, the white glare of searchlights, and the sweeping beams of high-powered flashlights lit up the night, reminding her a bit of the Las Vegas Strip. Their appearance was met with cheers.

Cooper cut the boat's motor as men in chest waders guided them in until the bottom of the boat scraped against the street pavement. Firefighters and EMTs swarmed, picking up the kids and assisting the women. One burly cop scooped up George and followed behind Mrs. Gonzales, assuring her that her dog was fine as the larger Lab waded to higher ground unaided. A game warden offered his hand to help Britt steady herself as she stepped out of the boat.

She scooted out of the way as Gil clambered out and headed toward a big white truck with a boat trailer. Cooper stayed in the boat, conversing with the man Britt guessed was the incident commander.

"No," she heard Coop say. "Gil and I didn't find anyone so I doubt anyone is left. Ms. Owens had this group in her truck and got caught in the backwash from the levee break." He removed his ball cap and scrubbed one hand over his face. His dark stubble glinted with a hint of auburn. He looked tired and she wondered how many rescues he and Gil had made.

The truck backed the trailer into the water and with expertise, Cooper guided the boat onto it. He climbed out, securing boat to trailer, and then walked beside it as Gil pulled away. A frenetic yowl caught everyone's attention. Malevolent yellow eyes glowered from an ink-black face. Cooper's gaze fell on her and she held her hands out in a no-clue gesture.

"The thing swam up and climbed on the roof of my truck," she explained.

Someone growled and she wasn't sure if it was cat or man. The two ended up in a stare-down. The cat blinked first. Britt was totally impressed. He continued to stare down the cat. "You gonna ride in the dang boat all night?"

She fought a laugh as the cat sprang from the boat, landed on Cooper's shoulder and hissed at anyone who came close. She knew just how the cat felt. She was even jealous of the darn thing because it was touching him. And yes, she was totally whacked. "Sleep deprivation," she muttered under her breath. As the men turned to walk away, she called, "Can I hitch a ride?"

Cooper glanced back at her and she had to suppress a shiver that had nothing to do with being wet or cold. *Nope.* The expression in his eyes warmed her from the inside out and she couldn't help but remember why she hadn't slept much the previous night.

"You want a ride?" His voice was like gravel rattling around in a velvet bag and his gaze was so intense she wondered if he had X-ray vision and could see that she'd gone commando that morning. She had to clear her throat before she could reply.

"Uh, yeah. That's why I asked. My truck's out of commission." She gave him a hopeful look. "I can still help. Besides, I don't have any place to go."

He'd rescued her more than once, and she felt as much a stray as the cat. Was he willing to offer her shelter again? She caught herself leaning toward him and straightened, which took far more effort than it should have.

"So," he drawled. "You want to help out?"

Yes, she wanted to help him out—help him out of those wet jeans that molded to his muscular thighs.

Memories of their night together flooded her and she wet her lips without considering the consequences—like his gaze turning molten as his eyes fixed on her mouth. A crooked grin quirked the corner of his mouth, right before he deflated her hopes.

"Fine. You can cat sit." He reached up, peeled the angry feline off his shoulder and placed it in her arms. He strode off, leaving her scrambling to catch up. Gil had the back door of the extended cab F-250 Ford open and he offered her a hand. Even with her long legs, it was a big step up into the back seat.

The cat scrambled out of her arms and settled next to the far door. It then began to thoroughly lick itself, ignoring the humans. Cooper climbed into the driver's seat, Gil in the passenger's. "Where're we goin' to, boss?"

"Your house."

The drive didn't take too long despite detours for flooded streets. Cooper kept glancing at Britt through the rearview mirror and smiled when she fell asleep. When they arrived at Gil's house, he slipped out of the truck with Coop's whispered instructions. "Get some sleep, Gil."

The man tossed him a roguish grin. "I be tellin' you the same thing, boss." He glanced into the back seat where Britt slept soundly. "You take that little gal home and you go to bed." Then Gil laughed softly, the sound slightly bawdy like he knew what Coop was thinking. Then he winked and stalked toward his wife, who was waiting for him on the porch.

Coop considered waking Britt enough to move her to

the front seat then left her alone. They were both running on fumes and he'd learned that you grabbed sleep whenever and wherever you could in an emergency. Luckily, Gil didn't live far from Barron Exploration Beaumont. When he pulled up to park at the field office, he was happy to see the large RV parked in the lot. Cord had come through for him by getting the RV delivered. It was far more comfortable than the air mattress in the break room. He climbed out and nudged Britt.

"Let's go, Girl Wonder."

Piercing yellow eyes glowered at him from the floorboards. Coop peered at the cat. The animal bared his fangs. "Got the feeling you're a devil cat. Guess I should call you Lucifer." The darn thing purred at him, the rumble so deep it sounded like a diesel engine. He laughed, which startled Britt awake.

She stared up at him with bleary eyes. "What's so funny?"

"Lucifer."

Her forehead crinkled and she looked so cutely confused, Coop was tempted to drop a kiss between her eyebrows. "Who?"

"The cat."

"Oh. What happens if it turns out to be a Lucy instead?"

He laughed again. "I wouldn't be surprised, with all that attitude. Serious diva territory."

Britt stirred, pushing stray strands of hair off her face, blinking the sleep from her fuzzy expression. "Where are we?"

"Home, sweet home. At least for the duration."

Britt gave him the fisheye and he fought not to laugh. “I have a hotel room calling my name.”

“One without electricity. My RV has lights, air conditioning and indoor plumbing.”

“You have a point.” She gripped his proffered hand to climb out. “Whoa!” She jerked and all but fell into his arms as the cat bolted across her shoulders and leapt to the ground.

Coop couldn’t help the smile tugging the corners of his mouth upward. She was an armful and he liked the feel of her next to him. Liked it a whole lot. She rubbed her eyes and gazed around. “What’s that?”

“My RV.”

She gave an appreciative whistle. “That’s not just an RV. That’s the Plaza Hotel of RVs.”

Coop led her over and opened the motor home’s door, standing back so she could enter first. She stopped dead. He looked over her shoulder, wondering why she wasn’t moving. He propelled her forward. “Showers. We need them. Then sleep, yeah?”

“Shower?” Britt’s eyes drooped and she looked completely exhausted.

“Right,” Coop muttered. He nudged her to the bathroom—and its full-sized shower. “You should grab the first shower and then hit the sack.”

“Uh-huh.”

“Britt?”

She shook herself and glanced up at him. “Right. Shower.” Glancing around, her gaze met his. They were both exhausted—and stank of bayou. Shower. Sleep. And tomorrow? Yeah, he’d do all the things he’d planned to do with her the previous morning, only to discover she'd skipped out on him.

"Do you need help?"

"Maybe." She sighed. "Okay, probably."

He stripped them both down, with far less attention to detail than he would have liked. He turned on the water and ushered her into the shower.

Britt was so tired she barely acknowledge the hands soaping her body. This could have been a lot of fun if she'd been alert and less exhausted because really? Cooper was a dream man.

She swayed a little on her feet. The next thing she knew, she was wrapped in a towel and on the bed. Cooper stood, a towel riding low on his hips, with his back to her. *Oh, boy.* Too bad she couldn't keep her eyes open.

"Big bed," she hinted, then yawned hugely.

"It is," he agreed. He pulled the covers over her and she thought the gesture was sweet. He slipped in beside her and she stiffened. With Cooper's very hard body next to her, she couldn't fall asleep. Then he snored softly. Britt relaxed, right into a deep sleep.

When Britt woke up, she kept her eyes closed. Controlling her breathing, she listened. She didn't remember where she was. Stiff, sore, still tired, with a headache nudging at the edge of her consciousness, she assessed her situation. Soft bed. Light filtering in through blinds. Warm body at her back. Muscular arm draped over her.

"Mornin', Girl Wonder."

Cooper. His voice sleep-roughened and as sexy as that hard length pressing against her butt. She was in so much trouble now, thanks to the happy dance her libido was doing. Clearing her throat, she mumbled, “Still sleeping.”

His body shook from laughter. Which translated into her body feeling things that made her want to turn, cup the man’s face and kiss him. With tongue. Despite morning mouth. What was wrong with her?

But the scent of this man and the warmth of his chest pressing against her back, the weight of his arm over her waist? Her mind was going there for sure. Then his lips nuzzled the back of her neck and she surrendered. Sort of. She had one tiny bit of fight left. “Are you trying to seduce me?”

His lips brushed across the shell of her ear. “Trying? No. I *am* seducing you. Is it working?”

Cocky man. She squirmed a little and his arm loosened just enough that the hand cupping her hip could propel her over onto her back. She gazed up at him, with his amazing blue eyes and a few days’ worth of stubble roughening his face. His lips were perfect—like an artist drew them. His brown hair showed hints of red where the sun caught it.

His fingertips stroked across her cheekbone before tracing her jaw. His gaze was focused on her mouth. “Yeah,” he breathed. “Definitely working.” Then he kissed her. Like he meant it. Lips and teeth and tongue. Searching, nipping, thrusting. Her heart rate kicked up and she melted against his bare chest.

Cooper chuckled against her mouth and she got a wild mental picture of his lips kissing another part of her body and what his laughter would feel like there.

Need and desire welled up inside her. The leash she normally kept on her control snapped. She hooked one leg over his thighs and pulled, making space for his hips between her legs. She rubbed against the hard length of his erection and threw caution to the wind. She'd seen so much destruction, the devastation created by both hurricane and flooding leaving people in desperate straits. She wanted another reminder that there was life and laughter and love. Right now, she just wanted to be a woman. Not a storm chaser. Not a weather reporter. Just a woman in the arms of a sexy man.

"Are we doin' this, Girl Wonder?" Cooper stared down at her, his body relaxed, his expression curiously hopeful.

"What happens if I say no?"

"I take a shower that will leave plenty of hot water for you. And if the cold shower doesn't work, I'll take care of business while I'm in there."

"Business?" she mused. "Do you consider this business?"

"No, ma'am. This..." He waved a hand between the two of them. "Is strictly pleasure. If *I* take care of things, then it becomes business."

"Ah." She strained to reach his mouth. He obliged by meeting her halfway. "Yeah," she whispered. "We're doin' this, Hero Boy."

"I'm not a boy." His hand cupped her beneath the sheet.

"And I'm not—" Her breath rushed out as he tweaked her nipple. "A girl."

He pushed the sheet down and a slow grin curled

the corners of his perfect mouth as his eyes crinkled. "I can see that."

A moment later, he was all over her—touching, cupping, teasing, kissing. His hands were work-roughened but not abrasive. A man with a manicure had never been her catnip. Cooper worked with his hands and she was definitely enjoying the way they worked her. Blunt fingers teased between her thighs, finding her already slick and ready. *This guy is not for you*, a little voice insisted. *It's bad for business. You need to get your tail in gear and get gone.* As his fingers teased her, she tuned out the voice. She wanted this. Him. For now, anyway. She pushed her hand between their bodies and latched onto his erection. He groaned into her mouth as his hand patted the small table next to the bed.

"Dammit, I know there's one in here somewhere," he muttered. "Gotta be."

Britt wondered what he was looking for when he let out a growl of triumph and she heard the sound of foil tearing. *Condom.* Good to know one of them was thinking.

When Coop rolled over to get the condom on, she noticed a deep scar running across his right thigh. Precaution in place, he started up where he left off—one hand stroking between her legs and his mouth taking her breast like he was starving and she was his favorite meal. He pulled away and looked into her eyes.

"Are you sure, Britt?"

No teasing now, because this much pleasure was serious business. "Yes."

She spread her knees as he rolled on top of her, bracing his upper body on his elbows and forearms. "Never thought I'd pull something so perfect from the flood," he murmured, dipping to kiss her again as he pushed inside.

Britt drew in a shuddering breath. Cooper did the same, then buried his face against her neck and exhaled. The previous night, they'd gone at it hot and heavy, but this? This was so much better. She clamped down on him as he thrust and withdrew, the friction of skin against skin igniting an astonishing awareness. Desire washed through her, seeking out every nerve and every cell of her body until she thought she would burn up.

Her thoughts scattered as sensation took over. Too difficult to think, or do anything but feel the hard length of him filling her. It was all so intense she couldn't form words, only make tiny noises as she spiraled up and up, reaching for something so profound, so all-consuming that she wanted to scream.

Braced on one arm, Cooper found the one spot that would release her frenzy with his fingertips. Moments later, her whole body arched off the bed and he caught her scream in his mouth as he kissed her with the same intensity. She held him tightly, fingers clutching, holding on. He thrust again and again, and then he groaned his own release and she felt him throb inside her.

He lay on top of her, spent, for several long minutes. Britt didn't care because breathing didn't seem all that important. The heat and feel of this man? Yeah, now that seemed crucial to her current well-being.

When he eventually rolled away, after a long and thorough kiss, she turned onto her side, hand tucked under her cheek. Eyelids heavy, she closed them until the bed shifted. With a yawn, she opened her eyes to focus on a very fine butt headed to the bathroom. A moment later, the shower kicked on. She found her watch and squawked. It was way past time to skedaddle. But she didn't have a vehicle and would have to wait on Cooper. Or find someone else to drive her back to the hotel.

Throwing on her clothes, she headed outside and found a small miracle—another storm team from Channel 2.

She plastered on a big smile and breezed toward where they stood talking to Gil. "Hi, guys. Time to go."

Three

Three months. He'd nursed his resentment for three months and there, standing across the ballroom, was the whole reason he refused to let bygones be bygones. Cooper hadn't wanted to come to this cocktail schmooze-fest billed as a fund-raiser for the University of Oklahoma School of Meteorology mobile tornado lab in the first place. Now, he wanted nothing more than to get out of the tuxedo and black tie his mother had forced him to wear. He and his six brothers might all be grown—well, except maybe Dillon, the baby of the family—but when Katherine Barron Tate arched a brow, her boys came to heel without a bark.

So here he stood, a watered-down whiskey in his hand, smiling politely at a weather geek waxing poetic about the revised Fujita scale and the need for more funding for research. Inside, Cooper was glowering at the beautiful blonde dressed in a sexy blue gown and surrounded by a herd of adoring sycophants. Yeah, so what if that was the word of the day on his secretary's desk calendar. It fit perfectly. Dragging his gaze away from the woman who'd starred in far more dreams than he cared to admit, he scanned the crowd for his mother. Locating her, he extricated himself from the one-sided conversation with the weather expert.

"Wow, that's awesome and all, but if you'll excuse me..." He didn't give the guy a chance to keep talking, ducking through the crowd toward Katherine. A man stopped him before he reached her.

"Well, if it isn't Cooper Tate. What are you doing here?"

Coop recognized an old fraternity brother. "Hey, Mark."

The man squinted at him as they shook hands. "I figured I was seeing things. A big oil tycoon like you mixing in with the science nerds?"

Coop glanced around to make sure his mother wasn't paying attention, then rolled his eyes. "It's Mom. This is her charity *du jour*. She was on the OU board of regents when the National Weather Service built their Severe Storms Lab down in Norman." He nodded toward a handsome man surrounded by a small crowd. "And I think she has a bit of a crush on Dave Edmonds from Channel Two. You?"

Mark made a face and said, "Somebody had to represent my law firm. I drew the short straw." He switched his expression to a smile as Katherine sailed up.

"Hello, Mark. How are your parents? Did they enjoy their cruise?"

How did his mother know all this stuff? It's like she kept a dossier on every person her sons had ever met. Or maybe she had his little brother Bridger on retainer, since Bridge worked for Barron Security Services.

"Mom's ready to sail around the world. Dad's still grousing about all the golf balls he launched into the ocean. He much prefers his eighteen holes on solid ground."

Mark and his mom continued to chat. Coop tuned them out. He'd never been one for small talk, especially not when it came to golf—Mark was bragging about being a scratch golfer, whatever that meant. Katherine appeared to hang on every word. Looking for a way to extract both of them, he touched his mom's arm. "I hate to interrupt but you'd mentioned something in the silent auction you wanted to bid on?"

She hadn't but if they were walking the long tables circling the room, they could pretend to be engrossed and he could avoid further conversation.

"So nice to see you again, Mark. Tell your parents I said hello."

Cooper nodded at the other man and steered his mother away.

"That was rude."

"You were as bored as me."

"One should always be polite in social situations, Cooper."

"Yes, ma'am." Agreeing with her was always easiest. "Oh, look!" He pointed out one of the items—a weekend at the Broadmoor Hotel in Colorado Springs. Katherine didn't stop so Coop trailed after her. When she did peruse an item, he pulled out his engraved Mont Blanc pen and added a bid to the sign-up sheet once she moved on. Then his mother stopped dead still and eagerly read an item's description. He came up behind her and read over her shoulder.

!!GO TORNADO CHASING!!

Why did graphics people put exclamation points in front of a header? More to the point, why was his mother so intrigued? He read the description. The high bidder would get to spend a day with a storm chaser from a local television station—one conveniently owned by his cousin Chase's company, Barron Entertainment. Who had time for that nonsense? Anyone who went looking for tornadoes was just plain loco in his book. Ever since his own up-close-and-personal experience with a twister when he was a kid, Coop was more than happy to give those suckers a wide berth.

Katherine raised her hand shoulder high and palm up. "Pen."

Cooper obliged. She accepted the pen and bent over the sheet, signed and added a ridiculously high bid. *Ouch.* He'd make sure his mother did *not* have the winning bid on this package, though he'd have to twist someone's arm to outbid her. Bridger was wandering around somewhere and he was an adrenaline junkie. Maybe he could talk his little brother into bidding. There was no way in hell he'd let his mom go.

He looked up and saw the picture attached to the description and read the caption beneath the woman's very attractive face: DANCE THE TORNADO TWO-STEP WITH BRITT OWENS. His mouth went dry. Britt Owens. Of course it would be her. Sexy-gorgeous even soaking wet and waiting for rescue from the top of her storm-chaser truck. Britt Owens, who sneaked away after incredible sex without a please, thank you or goodbye. Twice!

What was it about this woman? She obviously wanted nothing to do with him and yet he was drawn to her like iron to a magnet. So much for putting their encounter behind him because he was just wasting his time mooning after her, as his family reminded him often. He still wanted to kick himself for telling his brother, Bridger. The big blabbermouth. He was still staring at the picture when his mother elbowed him in the ribs. "Didn't I teach you not to drool?"

He blinked and by reflex, reached up to swipe at his chin—which was dry. "Dang, Mom. Seriously?"

She laughed, but he only managed to scowl before a local weatherman tapped the microphone on the stage, which caused ear-wincing feedback.

"Sorry about that," the man said with a laugh. "Those in charge informed me dinner will get underway just as soon as we all get seated. Once everyone is served, the entertainment portion of our evening will start. Trust me, this is a show you don't want to miss."

Without looking at how she'd signed the bid, Cooper offered his mother his arm and guided her to their table near the front. He seated her then sat on her left so they were both facing the stage but he could keep his eye on the rest of the room. He didn't like a bunch of strangers at his back. He wanted to see who was coming, but he also wanted to see the annual video they always aired. Maybe there'd be footage of Britt. Not that he cared.

Bridger slid into the chair beside him, a cocky grin on his face. "You still pouting over that little storm chaser?"

He glared at his younger brother. "I don't pout."

Okay, his mother *and* brother laughing at him? That hurt. And no way was his mother winning Britt's package. Nope. He was wise to Katherine Tate's ways.

Britt couldn't help herself. She sneaked by her package on the silent auction table to check the bidding. The last bid on the list was offered in a flowing, flowery script. Great. Just…great. One of the society ladies so prevalent in the room had decided to sign up for an adrenaline rush. She hated the whole idea of this package. Civilians didn't belong on the chase. They just got in the way and created problems.

Leaning over to study the page, Britt almost choked when she translated the signature into a name—and saw the four-figure bid amount next to it. Cooper Tate? *No. Just...no.* With furtive glances, she searched the room. What was he doing here? She knew he was a Tate, cousin to the Barrons who owned the TV station, but that didn't explain his presence at the gala.

Breathing through the semi-panic attack, she fought for composure. She'd made a crazy mistake last August down in Beaumont. Her face flamed with the memory and she quickly moved away from the auction table, worried about standing out. With luck, no one had noticed her agitation. As people found their seats, Britt headed toward the table sponsored by her television channel. She would not freak out. She couldn't afford to lose it, not with the station's chief meteorologist beaming at her. *Gah.* This whole fiasco had been his idea. The channel paid her more than her salary as an adjunct professor, so she needed to suck it up, buttercup.

She glanced at her watch as she arrived at the table. Three more hours. If push came to shove, she could always go hide in the ladies' room. The weeknight news anchor stood and held her chair. Britt sank into it and did her best not to fidget. The lights would dim after their food was served and with luck, she'd remain incognito. Salad plates filled with spring greens, tiny mandarin oranges and walnuts drizzled with balsamic vinaigrette waited at each place setting. Britt ate and listened as the station manager, the chief meteorologist and the anchor bantered back and forth. She didn't aspire to a career in TV. Nope. She wanted to finish her PhD then go into pure research. Though storm chasing and getting paid for it? Bonus!

Waitstaff in white shirts, their sleeves bunched with black garters, and wearing long black aprons, swirled through the tables deftly delivering artfully arranged plates. Once her table was served, conversation ceased and eating began. She cut into the pecan-crusted filet mignon, put the bite in her mouth and almost melted. The tender beef all but dissolved on her tongue. Herb-buttered new potatoes and steamed asparagus spears complemented the steak. Okay, the evening wasn't a total loss. She'd been expecting the usual rubber chicken so often served at events like this, even with a ticket price of a thousand dollars. The food she was enjoying with great relish was five-star all the way. Which was good, given her picky appetite these days.

The master of ceremonies took the stage and introduced the program—the history of storm chasing and the starring role Oklahoma, and the University of Oklahoma School Meteorology, played in the formation of tornado science. After inhaling the main course, Britt was unable to resist the chocolate mousse with raspberry dribble and a white chocolate tornado for garnish, spooning some into her mouth while her companions still finished their entrées.

She rolled her eyes at the good-natured ribbing as one of her segments splashed across the big screen behind the podium. A few of her graduate students wolf-whistled and she slouched in her chair as curious gazes focused on their table. Yes, indeed, the ladies' room was looking better and better. At the end of the video, the MC reminded people to bid and bid generously on the silent auction items. The lights came up and the cash bars reopened. A small musical combo began to play and people actually hit the dance floor.

When the anchor, a tall, broad-shouldered man, and his wife stood, Britt popped up beside them, and used them for cover, peeking around the barrier they formed to locate Cooper. No sign of him. That was bad. She needed to find him so she could avoid him at all costs.

The anchor glanced down at her and quirked a brow. "Problem?"

"Um…no." She twitched the flowing chiffon skirt

of her royal blue formal gown, her gaze tracking across the room. She stiffened as she found the object of her search.

The anchor's wife laughed. "If I were single, he'd be the kind of problem I'd want."

Oh, yeah. The man was devastatingly lethal in that black, Western-cut tux. The lapels and vest had a touch of shine under the lights and he wore a bolo tie with silver tips and a concho clasp. The hatband of his black Stetson had conchos too. And yup, there were shiny black Western boots on his feet. Britt stifled the sigh welling in her chest.

Dr. Garcia, the head of the university's meteorology department, chose that moment to arrive at their table. With everyone distracted, Britt finally beat a hasty retreat to the ladies' room. Several overstuffed chairs and something that resembled an antique fainting couch were grouped in the anteroom. Poking her head into the inner room, she made sure she was the only occupant before sinking into a chair. She was more than prepared to wait out the rest of the event right there.

You're being ridiculous, you know, her inner voice pronounced. *He probably doesn't even remember you.*

"Shut up," she muttered. "You don't know anything."

"I beg your pardon?"

Britt jerked her head up and stared at the woman who'd just walked through the door. She wore a lace and satin evening suit in rich cranberry. Attractive silver strands threaded through her short dark hair. A pearl-and-diamond necklace graced her neckline.

Blushing, Britt offered a sheepish smile. "Sorry. Talking to myself."

"I see." The woman paused a beat before adding, "You're Britt Owens."

"Yes, ma'am."

"I'm Katherine Tate."

Her stomach sank all the way to the floor, leaving behind a hollow spot that quickly filled with lead. Cooper's mother. Britt pasted a smile on her face and swallowed the spit swimming in her mouth. "Nice to meet you." Good. Steady voice. No panic. Yet.

Mrs. Tate's lips twitched but her rather stern expression didn't change. "So you chase tornadoes for a living. Must be thrilling."

"It can be. Thrilling. Yes. Mostly just boring though." Britt reeled off the statistical probabilities of a tornado forming in any given thunderstorm. Mrs. Tate nodded and looked moderately interested until Britt stopped babbling. "I mostly do it for research. I'm working on my PhD, you see."

"Fascinating," Mrs. Tate said as she looked Britt over from the top of her head to the freshly pedicured and red-painted toes peeking out from beneath her royal blue gown.

Britt swallowed hard, again, unsure just what it was the woman found fascinating—Britt's work or her as a person. Most people thought storm chasing was glamorous and exciting; surely that's what Mrs. Tate was referring to. So why did this woman terrify her far more than all the massive tornadoes she'd encountered?

Pushing to her feet, Britt locked her wobbly knees.

"So nice to meet you, Mrs. Tate. I should be getting back—" She gave a vague wave toward the door.

"Of course, dear. I'll see you again. Soon."

What did Mrs. Tate mean? There was something odd in her tone, a weight to the words Britt didn't understand. She pulled open the door and backed out, trying to decipher the implications of Mrs. Tate's parting words. She continued walking, all the while leaning to watch through the slowly closing door. Britt turned around just in time to plow into a hard body. Her forehead bounced off the muscled chest as her nose was buried in a starched shirt. Her instinctive inhale filled her lungs with the aromas of cardamom, bergamot and... She sniffed again. Was that lavender? What an intriguing mix of scents.

Strong hands gripped her biceps to keep her upright. She raised her chin, tilting her head back to look up. Straight into the frowning face of the last man on earth she ever wanted to run into.

"Cooper Tate!" someone shouted from behind him.

Coop turned his head to face the man who'd yelled his name. He didn't have time to duck the fist swinging at his face.

"You got my little sister pregnant."

Four

The sucker punch caught Cooper on the jaw and he went down like he'd been poleaxed. He was still holding onto Britt, his legs tangled in her skirts. As he fell, she had to follow. Hitting the floor was going to hurt so she braced herself—only to land on something hard but giving. Surprised speechless, she stared at the man standing over them, fists ready for a fight. Then his words sank in. *You got my baby sister pregnant.*

Their meaning had barely registered before camera flashes blinded her. She glanced at Cooper and winced. His face was already swelling and his eyes were unfocused. Still, he'd been careful to hit the floor in just such a way that she ended up cradled in his lap. She fought the melting sensation in the pit of her stomach as she pressed up against him.

"Get up!" Cooper's assailant ordered. "Stop hiding behind that—" A broad-shouldered man with a determined look jerked the guy away before he could finish his name-calling. Even though he wore a tuxedo, the newcomer could handle the physical stuff. Suddenly, there were more men surrounding her and Cooper, and Mrs. Tate, blocking them from onlookers and the barrage of cell-phone paparazzi.

Great. Just...great. The scrum of hard bodies consisted of Barrons and Tates. The tabloid media had dubbed the cousins Red Dirt Royalty. And Cash Barron's company owned the television station she worked for. Her career could end up in the dumpster due to this craziness. Defaulting on student loans wasn't on her bucket list and losing this job meant she might end up doing so. She needed to get away. Pronto. Before she could scramble to her feet, two sets of strong hands lifted her, steadied her, and then Mrs. Tate was hustling her back into the ladies' room. That worked—except that now she was once again all alone with her.

The door swished shut, muting the din out in the hallway. Britt grabbed her phone, immediately searching for evidence on social media of the catastrophe that just occurred. So far, her name hadn't been linked to it, but oh, yes, indeed, there were photos of Cooper's mug hitting the sites and lots of speculation. In the one picture of her sitting on his lap, she could only be identified by her dress and hair color, her face mostly blurred. Didn't matter how much the gown cost, she was burning it as soon as she got home. Problem was, she needed to ditch the dress before people remembered her wearing it.

"Breathe, Miss Owens," Katherine Tate ordered.

She'd forgotten the older woman was in the room. And Britt *was* close to hyperventilating. Cooper had gotten someone else pregnant? No, no, no, *no!* This wasn't happening. Part of her wanted to scream. Part of her wanted to cry. Most of her just wanted to run very far and very fast and pretend that this night had never happened.

"My sons and nephews will deal with the situation."

Britt opened her mouth to say something—anything—then snapped it shut. What exactly was there to say? Mrs. Tate apparently didn't notice. She bustled about, glancing at her phone when it pinged with incoming messages. The woman finally smiled as the outer door opened and a guy who looked a lot like Cooper, only a few years younger and several inches wider, entered, supporting Cooper with one of those broad shoulders braced under Coop's arm.

The man eased Cooper onto one of the overstuffed couches in the anteroom and gave his report. "Chance and Cash are dealing with the guy who cold-cocked Coop. Chase is dealing with the media. Cord is standing guard and diverting any of the ladies who might need the facilities. I think Jolie has gone in search of an ice pack. She'll be in to check on Coop shortly." He paused, giving Britt the once-over before returning his gaze to Mrs. Tate. "His storm chaser?"

"I do believe so, yes."

Hello. She was standing right here, and it was time to remind these people of that. She tried to speak for the second time just as the door popped open again.

A beautiful woman with chestnut hair and green eyes swept in, efficient and businesslike. She carried something bundled in a cloth napkin in one hand.

"Hey, Miz Katherine," she greeted the matriarch. "I brought ice. Move over, Bridger, so I can get a look at him."

The woman sat beside Cooper and Britt had to fight a stab of jealousy. Instead of thinking about that pretty woman's proximity to Coop, she attempted to figure out all the players without a program. She was familiar with the Barrons—Chase, Cash, Cord and Chance. There were two more Barron brothers, Clay and Kade, but as far as she knew, they weren't in attendance. Bridger had to be one of the Tates. The woman might be Jolene Barron, who was married to Cord. Wasn't she a nurse or something? Britt couldn't remember, but she was far too relieved by the large diamond wedding set on the woman's left ring finger.

"Wow, he nailed you good, Coop. Can you move your jaw?"

Katherine slipped out of the ladies' room, leaving her son to the tender mercies of her nephew's wife, the pretty storm chaser, and his younger brother. The hallway was clear but for Cord leaning against the wall. He straightened immediately.

"Aunt Katherine?"

"Stay here, Cord. Jolie will be out shortly. I want to look into something."

She steamed off without a backward glance. Pausing at the nearest entrance to the ballroom, she surveyed the area. The musical combo was playing and the dance floor was full of couples. Others strolled along the perimeter of the room checking on their favorite silent auction items.

A tall, impeccably dressed man stood in front of the display advertising Britt's item. Katherine watched as he perused the sign-up sheet, which was all he did, making no move to add a bid. She filtered through the crowd, keeping her eye on him. She'd first noticed him during the altercation outside the ladies' room. He'd been standing back, watching things with an air of aloof satisfaction. He looked vaguely familiar but not in that *he's-a-friend-of-my-boys* way. She'd figure it out eventually.

The man moved away, stopping at another item and she gave him time to get much farther down the line before she paused to double-check Britt's sheet. Excellent. Katherine still held the high bid—but she'd left it in Cooper's name. Which he hadn't noticed. So far, so good. She was tired of her son moping around because he was too proud to go after the woman he wanted. He needed a proverbial kick in the pants and spending time stuck in close proximity with that woman was just the ticket, even if it cost four figures.

Her nephew Cash caught her attention from where he stood near the entrance. She nodded toward him then began a roundabout meander in his general direction. She was halfway there when she heard her name.

"Mrs. Tate?"

She turned. The man who'd been so interested in

Britt's auction package stood a few feet away, smiling at her.

"Mrs. Katherine *Barron* Tate?"

Now wasn't that interesting, that emphasis he put on her maiden name. Her expression morphed into a very practiced and very polite smile. "Yes?"

"We've never met. I'm Alex Carrington."

Two things struck her. He emphasized his last name like she should recognize it and he watched her with an intensity that let her know he was extremely interested in her reaction to his surname. Her smile didn't change though she eventually quirked one brow. "Is there something I can do for you, Mr. Carrington?"

He dipped his chin and hesitated before speaking. "I only wanted to introduce myself so I could thank you for your patronage of the program."

Her cheeks plumped in a broader smile—one that did not reach her eyes. This man, who was older than he first appeared, was lying through his teeth. Without actually demanding his ID for verification, she'd estimate he was closest in age to Hunter, Boone or Cooper—her oldest three sons. And she *had* recognized his last name, though it was one she hadn't thought about in forty years. It was possible Alex was related to Colby. There were hints in the younger man's looks. Her one-time college beau had been handsome.

"Aunt Katherine?" Cash was at her side, his brother Chance coming up behind her as well. "Is there a problem here?"

She patted his arm, her smile now fond rather than chillingly polite. "None at all. Mr. Carrington was just thanking me for my sponsorship. Isn't that right, Mr. Carrington?"

The man eyed her nephews with disdain and she knew they didn't like his attitude from the way they stiffened, yet he answered with a very civilized, "Yes, ma'am. I won't keep you from the rest of your evening. Thank you again."

And with that, he was off, dodging through the crowd like he thought one of her nephews planned to follow and ambush him.

Cash took her elbow and steered her toward the nearest exit. "We need to talk."

"Of course we do, dear." She slipped one arm through Chance's and the other through Cash's. "And we have plans to make."

Cooper lay back on the couch, eyes closed, the ice pack firmly in place against his cheek and jaw. *His storm chaser.* That's what Bridger called Britt. And his mother knew. Of course she knew. Because Bridger had a big mouth. The conversation, what little there was, flowed over him. Until his brother nudged the armrest where his head lay.

"So, big bro. Baby daddy? Who's the lucky woman?"

He started to shake his head but stopped when stars danced on the backs of his eyelids and pain splintered his brain. *Ow. Reminder to self. Don't do that again.* "No clue," Coop muttered. "No clue who the dude is, or his sister."

"So who *have* you been seeing?"

Great. Bridger was in investigative mode. His brother would never shut up and go away now. "No one."

He caught the sound of someone snorting and cracked one eye open to see who. Britt. Yeah, he probably shouldn't have admitted that with her still in the room. She didn't need to know that he'd had no interest in any woman but her since coming home from Texas. And he wasn't about to tell her that he DVR'd the local news on the off chance she'd make an appearance. Pathetic. That's what he was. And the last thing he needed was for his brothers to find *that* out. They'd harass him unmercifully.

"The man who punched you seemed rather convinced." Britt managed to sound both annoyed and confident of the guy's right to throw a punch.

Cooper eyed his brother. "Maybe he confused me with one of you."

Rolling his eyes, Bridger laughed. "Hunter and Boone are in D.C. with Clay. Deacon and Tucker are both married. Dillon's been in Nashville. That leaves me, big bro, and don't even go there. I'm the stick-in-the-mud brother, remember?"

A second snort drew his attention to Jolie Barron, Cord's wife. "Pah-lease, Bridge. I'm wearing expensive heels and not a pair of hip boots in sight. You might be able to fool your mom and brothers but the rest of us?" She waggled an index finger at the younger man before blowing him a kiss.

The door opened and two giggling girls breezed in. They stopped dead, staring, gazes darting between the occupants. Coop groaned inwardly.

"I do believe that's our cue to skedaddle," Britt announced. "I'm not sure of the decorating scheme in the men's room, but surely there's a chair in there you can occupy while you sulk."

She was out the door before Cooper could say anything to stop her. The two girls parted like the Red Sea, though their gazes remained fixed on him and Bridge. Working his jaw gingerly, he sat up with only a little assistance from his brother.

"Don't mind us, ladies," Bridge announced as he hauled Coop to his feet.

Jolie insisted Coop keep the ice pack on his face and she pushed up under his shoulder. Still seeing more stars than he was comfortable with, he leaned on Bridger, too, as soon as they were out the door. Once his vision cleared, he searched the hallway for Britt. She'd disappeared. His brother and Jolie, followed by Cord, steered him toward a small sitting area in an alcove and settled him into one of the chairs.

"You were supposed to keep people out, Cord," Jolie scolded. "Especially people of the female variety."

"Like some random guy is going to push his way into the ladies' room?" Cord did an exaggerated eye roll. "My cousins being the exception to that rule. What went on in there and why are you not chasing the storm chaser? She's hot. Also, what the hell, cuz? You're having a baby?"

Jolie glared at Cord while speaking to Coop. "Keep the ice on your face, Cooper. I *will* be keeping track." She turned on her heel and crooked a finger at her husband. Cord followed willingly.

Bridger waited until the couple was out of earshot before dropping into the chair next to Cooper. "She's bad news, big bro."

"You don't even know her."

"Nope. Just what I've seen of her on TV. But I've got good instincts and my gut says she's going to bring you nothing but trouble."

Before he could argue, Bridge continued. "I know what went on down in Beaumont. I know what you've been like since you got home."

"You don't have a—"

"Dude, she left you. Twice."

Five

Cooper scowled at his brother's retreating back. Technically, Bridger was correct. Britt had ditched him without saying goodbye. Twice. After they'd made love. Well, maybe not…love. Wild monkey sex. Still, it was the best sex he'd ever had and there was something about the damn woman that aroused all sorts of deep-seated feelings inside him. She was bold and beautiful.

If his face didn't hurt so bad, he'd bang his forehead on the side table. Wasn't that the name of some soap opera his mom watched? He didn't have time for drama. He worked for a living. And Bridge was right. While he wasn't the ladies' man of the Barron-Tate clan, he didn't have to sit home twiddling his thumbs because the object of his affection chose to ignore him. There were plenty of fish in the sea. Only he didn't want tuna.

He wanted filet mignon. His stomach chose that moment to growl. Not surprising since he'd been too busy watching Britt to eat much. He vaguely remembered beef. And potatoes. Yeah, he was hungry.

For Britt. The remembered taste of her settled on his tongue. What was it about her that heated his blood? Bold and beautiful, he reminded himself. There was something about her nerdy glasses, the scientific language. Who knew that a one-sided discussion of quasi linear convective systems made for good pillow talk?

And now this whole crazy allegation that he'd impregnated some girl. His accuser had been arrested and hauled off in handcuffs. What was Britt thinking? He wasn't reckless when it came to unprotected sex. Denver Tate had drilled that lesson into his sons' heads over and over. No condom, no sex. He didn't lose control and forget.

Britt probably thought he was a total bastard. Given the circumstances, he couldn't blame her. He closed his eyes and rubbed at his sore jaw. Then again, why would she care? She'd gotten out of his bed and walked away. Twice.

"Idiot," he muttered, before his thoughts were interrupted by a burst of applause. They were announcing the silent auction winners. Crap. He'd meant to fix his mother's bid. Too late now. He sighed, resigned to dealing with his mother when the time came to chase tornadoes with Britt. He considered slinking out of the museum and taking himself home. Bridger could give their mother a ride to her house when the event was over.

Reaching up, he tugged on his bolo tie and undid the

collar button strangling him. He shifted the ice pack, not quite ready to abandon its cold comfort. Yeah. He'd go to his truck, text his brother and head home. That was a good plan. Right after he put Britt Owens out of his mind.

Coop heaved out of the chair and glanced around, furtive in his movements. If any of his family lurked about, his plan would fall apart. The coast was clear. He slipped outside into the cool autumn air and paused, inhaling deeply. Beyond the entrance portico, glittering stars scattered across the night sky. Something eased in his chest. He was a country boy at heart. When it came to life in the big city with tall buildings, bright lights and traffic, sometimes it was hard to breathe but clear, crisp nights like this one helped him cope.

He headed across the parking lot toward his truck and stopped dead. Right in front of him, wrapped in decals touting KOCX TV's weather team, sat Britt's chase truck. Fate had to be working overtime. Or karma was about to rise up and bite him in the butt. He could just keep walking, get in his truck and drive away. Or, he could admit that Britt had gotten under his skin and he wanted her like he'd never wanted another woman.

His dad had taught his sons another important lesson. Don't be a quitter. Britt's actions had bruised his ego. He could admit that. But he wasn't a quitter. And he didn't run away. Time to make a stand.

Leaning against the push bars on the front bumper of Britt's chase vehicle, he settled in to wait. He was taking a big gamble but if things worked out, he'd reap a reward that would make everything worth it. There was just something about the woman that made him want to risk everything to keep her.

Unable to get her out of his head for the last three months, he'd been plotting ways to cross her path. In retrospect, the series of unfortunate events tonight leading up to him laid out in the women's lounge with Britt for company was a good thing. And yeah, he was probably a pathetic excuse for a single guy but he didn't care. The woman checked off every item on his list. Until he got her out of his system, he'd continue being in danger of losing his man card.

Better to confront the situation head-on. Even better would be getting his hands and mouth on her again. Things stirred inside him. This was nothing serious. Just chemistry. And just until he got bored with her. That was his story and he was sticking to it.

"Stupid shoes," Britt groused as she switched heels for the flip-flops she'd stashed in her evening bag. Her feet and ankles were swollen and sore. Holding her skirts off the floor, she headed for the exit with one thought in mind: get home. Her feet hurt. Her back hurt. And if she stopped to think about it, her heart hurt far more than it should. She knew what she had to do to be fair but after that scene tonight? How could she share her news with Cooper?

A few people spoke to her as she walked outside and she waved at them without speaking. No time for conversations. If she got detoured, Cooper might find her. Or not. Was he even looking for her? She didn't want to see him. Nope. Not at all. So why was she feeling depressed that he hadn't hunted her down?

"On the fence much?" she muttered to herself as she arrived at the asphalt parking lot. Some sixth sense had her raising her head to peer into the spotty shadows. A figure leaned against the front of her truck. A tall, lean figure, with booted feet crossed to match those arms across his muscled chest. Her idiotic heart fluttered with excitement. He *had* tracked her down. But she wasn't ready to talk to him. Not yet. Not until she found out more about that guy who'd ambushed Cooper. And the guy's pregnant sister. Because at the moment, no matter how much he set her heart on fire, if he was guilty as charged? No. She couldn't think about that other woman. She had to keep her wits about her to deal with him.

"Howdy, Girl Wonder." Why did his deep drawl have to sound so sexy? And why did it send shivers through all the feminine places in her body?

"Fancy meeting you here, Hero Boy." She wanted to kick herself for falling so effortlessly into their familiar flirting.

"I keep tellin' you, I'm not a boy."

She tilted her chin up and watched him through half-lowered lashes. "Coulda fooled me." She waited a beat then added, "Quite a scene tonight."

Did he blush? "I have no clue what that guy was talking about."

"Of course you don't." Sarcasm. Good. She could use sarcasm.

"You don't believe me." He gazed up at the stars. "Of course you don't."

Interesting. He could do sarcasm too. Good to know.

Cooper shoved his hands into his trouser pockets. "Look, this happens."

'What? You being accused of—"

"Yes." He cut her off. "People accuse my cousins and us of all sorts of things."

She knew that, yet she'd still been quick to judge.

"And due to those kinds of accusations, we are always extremely careful."

Not careful enough, she mused.

When he lifted his hand and cupped her cheek, she didn't back away. He stepped closer, lowered his head.

"I've missed you," he whispered against her lips.

She didn't fight him when he deepened the kiss. She should have, but truth be told, she'd missed him too. "What are you doing?" she murmured against his mouth. He didn't answer, not in words, but he pulled her closer, claiming her with the heat of his body and intensity of his kiss.

"Taking you home," he finally replied.

"This is my truck and I'm perfectly able to drive."

"Let me rephrase that. I'm taking you home with me."

Her brain processed his statement. Home with him? To his house? *Cooper* was trouble. She was walking and talking proof of that. And in all probability, he was somebody's baby daddy. *Somebody else's* baby daddy. And that thought hurt far more than it should, given the circumstances. She didn't know him. Didn't have a claim on him. Didn't want one. Nope.

Then he kissed her again. Every bit of good sense she possessed skipped out on her, like some carefree girl tromping through the tulips. She kissed him back, her arms snaking around his neck.

"Please," he murmured against her ear. "Come home with me."

They could talk there, with no one around to hear or see them. She wasn't ready. Not yet. Not with this other accusation hanging over his head but things still needed to be said.

Listening to her heart instead of her head, she agreed. Still, she was not going to be stuck without a ride. "Okay, but I'm driving."

"We'll take your truck but I'm driving. You don't know where I live." He held out his hand, palm up. "Keys?"

She dug in her clutch muttering about alpha males but she handed them over. He beeped the locks and helped her into the passenger seat. Before she could have second thoughts, the man who stole all her good intentions with a look was in the driver's seat. They didn't go far. Out of the parking lot, along 63rd Street, and a quick left onto a private drive with an electronic gate. The drive curved through trees and then opened up to a broad lawn. Perched atop a low hill, the house was a complete surprise with its buff-colored native stacked stone and metal roof gleaming beneath the moon.

Cooper parked, was out, and had the passenger door

open. Too late to change her mind. The interior of his house was just as impressive as the exterior.

"You want a drink?"

"No, I'm good."

A grin that quirked one corner of his mouth. "As I recall, you're very good."

He walked into the kitchen and grabbed a frosty bottle of water from the fridge. He took a moment to open it and drink deeply.

"I know what you're thinking," he finally said.

Her hand convulsively curved around her stomach. There was no possible way but she nodded.

"Look, Britt. I'm a Tate and two of my brothers are country music stars. I'm also a Barron on my mom's side. That means money. A lot of it. False paternity suits are a thing."

"And I should believe you?"

"Yes." He looked so earnest. "My dad raised us to be responsible. I haven't been—" He cut off whatever he was about to say. "You'll just have to take my word for it."

Deep down, and for obvious reasons, she wanted to believe him. He slowly walked toward her, setting the bottle down on the bar as he passed it.

"I've missed you, Girl Wonder."

Then his arms were around her and he was kissing her again. She pushed against his chest and broke the kiss, studying his face.

"I'm not the love 'em and leave 'em type, Britt."

He wasn't. She knew that on a level that scared her just a bit.

"Will you stay with me tonight?"

How could she refuse? And why would she want to. She kissed him, just a brush of her lips across his. "Okay."

He led her into a very masculine, very Cooper bedroom. A wall of windows looked out over the lights of Oklahoma City. The massive bed was dark wood with padded leather head and footboards. She could get lost in that bed.

He was kissing her again, his hands caressing her sides and back, her arms. She was suddenly too hot but goose bumps prickled her skin. She pulled at his shirt but it barely came untucked. He continued to kiss her while he stripped out of his tux jacket and vest. Then she heard cloth ripping and small pings. Had he ripped his shirt open?

Strong fingers found the zipper of her dress and in moments, it lay in a billowing pile around her feet. He picked her up and laid her down gently on the bed. Then Cooper was lying beside her, his hands and mouth roaming over her body.

Britt knew in her head that she should stop this but the chemistry between them short-circuited her logic, because her heart? Yeah, her heart wanted what was about to happen. So did her body. Surrendering to the inevitable, she turned into him and pushed the shirt off his shoulders before busying herself with his belt and trousers.

Just like the other times they'd been together, they were naked in no time at all. The man knew precisely how to tease her with his hands and his mouth; knew the exact places to touch and kiss and suck to send her flying hard and fast over the edge.

Now it was her turn. With a touch here, a kiss there, she had him flying. He groaned and before she could react, he'd flipped them so he was on top. He spread her legs and his sexy, half-lidded eyes drank her in. Then he was sliding inside her.

She shuddered around him, clutching at his shoulders as he pushed deep. "Yes," she murmured. "Oh, yes, please."

What seemed like hours later, groggy and sated, she snuggled in with her head and half her body draped across his muscular torso. Cooper had just enough hair on his chest to pet and her fingertips ruffled through the dark, copper-colored wisps. Her muscles felt like butter left in the sun and she could barely keep her eyes open. She wasn't spending the night. Doing so was dangerous. Tears prickled behind her lids and she cursed her volatile emotions. She had to get a grip. Her life was about to get even crazier. Coop deserved an explanation but she just wasn't ready especially in light of the things he'd said earlier. Despite her mixed feelings, his steady heartbeat beneath her ear and the rise and fall of his chest made her feel safe. *I'll rest for just a minute*, she decided. *Until I'm sure he's asleep. Then I'll go.*

Britt blinked awake. How long had she been asleep? Beyond the windows, night lightened to the dove gray of predawn. The man beside her snored softly. Good. He was still asleep. Time to go. Easing out of bed, she located her clothes—draped over a large leather armchair next to the bed. She didn't bother with anything but the dress. Undergarments could wait. She noticed one set of windows was actually a French door. She could slip outside and go directly to the driveway where her truck was parked.

Hesitating, she glanced back at the bed. The sleeping man lay on his back, one arm stretched to the side. The arm, she realized, that she'd been sleeping on. His hair was tousled and scruff shadowed his jaw and cheeks. He looked so handsome, so… No. Britt shook those thoughts right out of her head—literally. Cooper Tate was not hers. Not that she'd want him. She didn't need a man and while some female *might* try to trap a man, she wasn't *that* woman. Not after the accusations of the previous evening. Her heart believed his explanation. Her head? Nope. Her head was such a pessimist.

She now regretted shaking her head. She was already feeling too queasy for her peace of mind. She would not throw up here. It was time to make her escape. As she eased the door closed behind her, she couldn't resist taking one last look at the man who might have been hers. Under different circumstances, in a different time and place.

She'd have to talk to him eventually—tell him—but not today. Not after last night. Squaring her shoulders, she turned away, resolute. Time to go.

Cooper didn't move, didn't open his eyes, as he listened for the sound that had first awakened him. The weight on his chest moved. But it wasn't Britt, it was the damn cat.

The bed beside him was still warm. Maybe the noise was Britt in the bathroom. He waited for her to come back to bed. After a few minutes with no further sound, he glowered at Lucifer until the cat moved, then threw off the covers and stalked to the en suite bathroom. It was empty. Nothing had been touched. The sink was dry. Weird. He availed himself of the facilities before heading back to the bedroom. He rummaged in his dresser for a pair of boxers then looked around.

Her dress was gone, along with the frilly things she'd worn underneath. He stalked out, headed to the kitchen. It was too much to hope that she'd be there fixing coffee. The kitchen was pristine. His housekeeper had been there just yesterday and he'd come home from the office, showered, donned his tux, and headed to the Western Heritage Museum for the benefit. Which reminded him. He'd need to get dressed and hike over there to pick up his truck. Good thing he basically lived across the street from the museum.

Lucifer demanded breakfast so Coop poured out some kibble and added a couple spoonfuls of wet food. He set the cat's bowl on the floor and then got to the important stuff. Coffee. He poured a pot of water into his coffeemaker and snagged a mug while it brewed. Then he got the bright idea to check his security system. Not that he'd taken the time to arm the house last night. He'd barely had the presence of mind to disarm it, and that only because he didn't want to be interrupted by phone calls or knocks on the door. Barron Security was nothing if not thorough. And knowing his little brother, had the alarm gone off, Bridger would have been the one showing up and standing there in the doorway with a cocky grin on his face.

He swiped the electronic tablet on the breakfast bar that separated the kitchen from a large family room as he settled on one of the bar stools. Running the video feedback, he watched as they arrived the previous night. The feed followed him through the house, carrying Britt, but cut off at his bedroom. The next motion-activated camera clicked on at 6:26 a.m. The sky outside was still dark but traces of gray showed on the eastern horizon. Outside lights, triggered by Britt's movements, clicked on and he followed her around the corner to the driveway. She climbed into that monster truck of hers, started it and got it turned around so she could head down the drive. The cameras mounted on the gateposts at the street showed the metal gate sliding open at the approach of her truck, closing once she was clear. The last look he got was the rear of her truck as she pulled out onto 63rd Street and drove off.

"Note to self," he muttered. "Kill the pressure plate in the drive and put in a code pad." If he'd had that, she wouldn't have been able to get away. Again. He had to be the world's biggest glutton for punishment. Except the heat between them was enough to scorch the eyebrows off anyone standing too close.

Three times. They'd been together three times and he'd given her multiple orgasms. So why did she keep skipping out on him? His morning breath couldn't be that bad.

How many times would he watch her sneak away before he got smart? He was known to be stubborn but this whole deal had finally reached a level of absurdity even for him. He should cut his losses.

"Third time's the charm," he groused. His brother was right. He was cursed. And he was done. Britt Owens was not the only smart, sexy and totally fascinating woman in the world. Too bad she was the only one who kicked up a storm in his heart.

Six

Lost in his thoughts, Cooper was paying no attention that Monday morning when the Barron Tower elevator doors slid open and he took one step into a wall of muscle. His boss, Cord Barron, stiff-armed him back into the elevator car. Cord's brother Chance and Bridger joined them as the doors whispered shut. Bridger stabbed the button for the thirty-fourth floor, where Barron Security had offices.

"Somebody wanna fill me in on what's going on?"

The other three men simply stared at him. The car stopped, the doors opened, and two secretaries got on. Cord and Chance were both married but that didn't stop the women from checking them out before their gazes came to rest on Cooper and Bridger. That's when the flirting started. Bridge indulged. Cooper didn't. He was still steamed over Britt's disappearing act Saturday morning. As a result, he was annoyed with the entire female half of the population.

Thankfully, the women were headed to a different floor and stayed on when the elevator got to thirty-four and the men exited. He pretended not to hear the sighs and titters as the doors closed. Coop hunched his shoulders and followed the others through the impressive reception area of Barron Security.

"Still wanna know why I'm here," he muttered.

"You'll find out as soon as Mom gets here."

He furrowed his brows, staring at his younger brother. "Why is Mom coming into town?"

"Because this is her deal, according to Cash."

"Then why are Cord and Chance here?"

"Because Mom's involved." Bridger's tone implied that Coop was a simpleton. He didn't add the implied *well, duh*.

A low hum of activity followed them down the hallway to the executive offices. Cheri, Cash's personal assistant, handed everyone a cup of coffee as they passed the side bar on the way to Cash's office. A huge black dog lunged off the leather couch, barking happily as his tail cut through the air like an old-fashioned fan. The Newfoundland, belonging to Cash's wife, Roxie, greeted everyone before returning to his spot on the couch.

"Take your dog to work day?" Chance asked, smirking.

Cash rolled his eyes. "You try telling Harley he can't go for a ride."

As the men settled in the sitting area with their mugs, Coop remained standing. He wasn't out of the loop very often and the fact he was this time irritated him to no end. Considering everything that had happened Friday night, he'd been expecting his family to get all up in his business. They didn't. Which was unusual. So maybe they'd just been biding their time, gathering the facts, and were now ready to ambush him. Yeah, that's probably what this was.

His fingers brushed over the bruise on his face, compliments of the crazy dude who'd accused Coop of getting his sister pregnant. Except Coop hadn't been with anyone. Well, he'd been with *someone…*

Coop wanted to kick his own ass. He had to stop thinking about Britt. She was old news. They'd had an unfortunate series of one-night stands. They didn't have a relationship and since she ditched him after each encounter, they didn't have a future. It didn't matter that her sexy scientist vibe turned him on. He shifted uncomfortably, his body reacting to the memory of making love to her.

His mother chose that moment to breeze through the door. She made the rounds, doling out cheek kisses to all, sons and nephews alike. She held up a finger, freezing Harley as he sat up in preparation for an exuberant greeting but ruffled the dog's ears to show him he was still loved. Then she sank into a deep leather armchair, reigning like a queen.

Her gaze pinned first Bridger, who was bringing her a cup of coffee, and then Cash. "So," she said, accepting the cup. She sipped, swallowed. "Did you find out anything?"

Cash deferred to Bridger, who gave a brief rundown. "Alex Carrington, full name Alexander Adam Carrington, is from Hartford, Connecticut. He graduated from Harvard with a BS in business. He's a vice president of CCI, Ltd. As near as we can figure, CCI is some sort of holding company. His father is Colby Carrington the third."

"Trey."

Bridger continued to drone on about parentage, stepmothers and siblings, and Coop figured he was the only one who caught the breathy word his mother uttered. This whole conversation caught him off guard. He'd figured this was an ambush about the alleged pregnancy and/or Britt. But there was way more going on.

He watched his mother, noticing the hard glitter in her eyes. She was edging toward angry. It took her a long time to blow her stack but when she lost her temper, people ran for cover.

"He bought his ticket to the fund-raiser six weeks ago, when it was announced," Bridger continued. "We don't know why he is here or why he would approach—"

"I know," Katherine announced. "I want to know about the other things I asked you to look into."

This time, Cash deferred to Chance, the senior partner of the Barron law firm. "The guy who attacked Cooper—and nice shiner you got there, bud—has no criminal record. He was arrested and released on his own recognizance." He looked back at Cooper. "You know a guy named Steve Maddox?"

Coop shook his head. "No clue who the dude is."

"How about Susan or Susie Maddox?"

"Nope."

"That's his sister and she's claiming that you're the father of her unborn child."

Hands fisted, Coop came off the wall where he'd been leaning and made it two steps before Chance stopped him. "I've confirmed she is pregnant."

"I didn't—"

"Of course you didn't, Cooper," his mother interrupted. "Your father and I taught you boys better. Hear your cousin out."

Chance nodded to Katherine before focusing once more on Coop. "I've also confirmed that she had a live-in boyfriend and that he moved out when she told him she was pregnant. Apparently, she's filing a paternity suit naming you. As soon as she does, I'll be filing papers with the court demanding a prenatal paternity test, along with costs and damages when her claim is proved false."

He walked a file over to Coop and handed it to him, a photo on top. "Be positive you don't know her, Coop."

Britt huddled into a chair at a table in the corner of the bright room. Every kind of soda pop bottle imaginable lined the walls of Pops 66. People at the other tables were enjoying all manner of roadside diner food and soda pop. Why she'd thought this was a good place to meet Ria Simms, the morning on-air meteorologist at Channel 2 and the closest thing to a best friend she had, escaped her at the moment. The food aromas made her stomach queasy and the ginger ale she'd ordered wasn't helping. The other woman breezed up and slid into the chair opposite her.

"You look like crap," Ria announced with a big smile. Her sunny disposition was perfect for the early newscast. Britt was not a morning person and perky just didn't help her mood, all things considered.

"Can you tone down the cheerful?"

"No. Besides, that's why you called me. You always call me when you're feeling down."

A waitress arrived, took Ria's order, and disappeared.

"How can you eat a double bacon cheeseburger at ten in the morning?" Britt's stomach lurched at the thought.

"I've been at work since four a.m. This is like noon to me. Don't worry. I'll share my fries."

Britt held up a hand, feeling more than a little green. "No. Don't do me any favors."

Dropping her voice, Ria turned serious. "So it's like that, huh? I remember those days. How far along?"

She held up three fingers and then wiggled a fourth. She could all but see the wheels turn in Ria's head and quickly preempted the other woman's question. "Don't ask how it happened."

"Fine. Then who's the father?"

"Don't ask."

"So I can't ask how and I can't ask who. Guess it's a good thing I do the weather instead of hard news." Ria paused while her drink was delivered. When the waitress was out of earshot, she said, "Well, whoever he is, have you told him yet?"

Britt didn't answer, suddenly fascinated by the bubbles in her glass of ginger ale.

"If you know who—"

"Of course I know who!" Britt was furious that Ria would even consider she didn't.

The other woman held up both hands to temper Britt's anger. "Down, girl. Wasn't insinuating you didn't. I was simply predicating my question. Since you know who, why haven't you told him?" Her eyes widened. "Oh, no. Please don't tell me it's someone at the station."

"It's not." Just a relative of the owner. Britt felt even more nauseous.

"Whew!" Ria swiped the back of her hand across her forehead to emphasize her relief at that news. "So what's the problem?" She blinked. "Oh, goodness. He's not married, is he?"

That earned her a growl from Britt. "Who do you think I am, Ria?"

"Well, I didn't figure you for someone who would get involved with a married man, but some of the men I know can be both slick and sneaky about stuff like that. I've had friends get caught in their traps."

While Ria ate her burger, Britt found herself inexplicably telling the whole story. Of the life-altering events in Beaumont, the need—and hunger—for a human connection. Of the off-the-charts chemistry between her and Coop, without naming him. And the fact that she'd been with him three times and had taken off without saying anything much less goodbye all three times. She let slip about the incident at the benefit and covered her mouth in shock as Ria did the same.

"Dudette! Do not tell me that you were in the middle of that..." Ria blinked rapidly. She grabbed her smartphone, did a search and scrolled through the pictures that popped up. "You *were.* I recognize your dress now. How you managed to keep your face out of those pictures..." She glanced up, stared. "It's a freaking miracle you weren't identified."

"Yeah, I know. Totally lucky. But here's my dilemma. I know I have to tell him. Well, I don't really have to—" She held up her hand to stave off Ria's argument. "I *don't have* to tell him. Not too ethical on my part if I don't. But at the same time, here's this bimbo who's also having his baby. I mean, it's not like I want to marry him or anything."

Except she had daydreamed what that would be like on more than one occasion. And now that she'd seen where he lived? *Wowser.* His house was perfect. She didn't think she could sit down and plan a house that fit her any better than his, at least from the parts of it she'd seen. And there was that zing of electricity that ignited whenever they touched.

But chemistry didn't equal love. And given the current situation, he might think she was just another gold digger.

"So you're worried that he'll think you did this on purpose to get his money?"

She tuned back into the thread of conversation, shocked Ria's thoughts paralleled her own. "What?"

"Britt, Cooper Tate is rich. I mean, serious money.

His mom is a Barron, and half the Tate boys work for the Barron brothers. Then there's Deacon, who's a megastar in Nashville. I know for a fact that all of the Barron brothers have had at least one paternity suit filed against them." Ria tilted her head. "Except they were all proved false. Well, except for Cord. That whole story never made it into public domain, but there's no doubt that Jolene Davis's little boy is his. All you have to do is look at the two of them side-by-side. That kid is his dad's mini-me. Anyway, people are always trying to get their hooks into the Barrons and the Tates to get at their money."

"I don't want his money."

"I know that. But, hon, it takes two to make a baby and having a village to help raise it is a big help."

"He used condoms." Well, he had until last night. Of course, the horse was already out of the barn by then.

"And condoms break." Ria laughed, the sound as bright and breezy as her personality. "That's how Tick and I ended up with our first." She reached across and patted Britt's arm. "Honey, I know this is hard, but there's a couple of things you need to consider. One, as the biological dad, he has a right to know, and to take part in any discussions pertaining to—"

"No. I've already decided to keep the baby."

"Okay, okay. I figured, considering you're coming out of your first trimester. But have you considered the monetary side of things? Yes, we have good insurance at the station, and liberal maternity leave, but it's expensive to have a kid. As the biological father, he should be responsible and help pay medical costs and child support."

Ria was right. Britt knew that deep in her heart, but honestly, she was terrified of Cooper's reaction, especially coming on the heels of Friday night. That guy hitting him and claiming Coop had gotten his sister pregnant? *Crazy sauce.* And now for her to drop her little bombshell into the conversation, considering how many times she'd taken the chicken's way out and bailed on him? He was going to hate her. And she *could* raise this child alone. Her dad had done it with her and her little brother, after her mother took off. She could, too, because she really didn't want to be tied down to a man like Cooper Tate.

"You need to talk to him, Britt."

Squinting her eyes shut, she exhaled. "Yeah, I know."

"And the sooner the better."

Yeah, she'd get right on that. Not.

Seven

Fed up with civilization and the machinations of the female half of the human race, Cooper was relieved to have business that took him out of Oklahoma City. BarEx was drilling a new well down in the Anadarko Basin. Thanksgiving at his mom's had been a full-court press from his family. He hated being the center of attention, but at least everyone was on the same page. That whole deal at the gala had been a setup.

Before leaving the office, he'd changed into old jeans and a ratty T-shirt, though he also pulled on a polo shirt bearing the company logo—the clothes he usually wore when working in the oil patch. He planned on spending the rest of the day playing roughneck, getting his hands dirty. He had hopes the hard work would drive the thoughts of both the woman trying to trap him with her false claims and the woman he wanted to entice back into his bed out of his brain.

Music from his brothers' latest album filled the cab of his pickup truck. Deacon and Dillon had gotten all the musical talent in the family. He couldn't carry a tune in a bucket and he'd driven the piano teacher his mother hired to teach him the basics to the nearest liquor store for a bottle of wine. But he could play ball—football *and* baseball, though not well enough for a D-1 school, much less the pros. Nope, he was just happy hunting, fishing and working on the ranch in his spare time.

Growing up on the ranch, he paid attention to the weather and its effects on operations. Last spring, they'd had record rains, followed by one of the driest summers and falls on the record books. Rain in the spring meant lots of green growing things. Summer and fall droughts meant dead things in the fields just ripe for catching fire. Driving along, he noticed all the red cedars and acres of dried grass filling the fields and pastures stretching along the section line road he followed to get to the well site. An early hard frost, especially after a summer and fall with little rainfall, made for a prime fire season. Except it was late November—an unseasonably hot and dry November.

Drilling an oil well was dangerous business under the best of circumstances. The scars on his legs were a testament to that. He and Cord had both been injured on a rig. Cord had almost died. Coop would have but for Cord's intervention. Since coming out of the hospital and off physical therapy, he'd made it his mission to make sure every well site and field office was as safe as possible. Given his childhood brush with a tornado, that included contingencies based on whatever the local weather could throw at them.

The site appeared on his right and he slowed to turn onto the access road they'd cut into the rancher's field. His truck rattled over the cattle guard and he eyed the site. The immediate area had been cleared and graveled. A retention pond held water and an overflow pond was lined and ready for drilling mud once they got to that point. The rig was in place, as were the propane and diesel tanks for fuel. A familiar figure stepped out of the doghouse—the control center for the rig.

Deja vu, Coop thought. Tom Bradley had been the toolpusher on the rig where he and Cord had been hurt. He'd worked with the man several times over the ensuing years and seldom thought back to that incident. Why, on this day, his head was tripping down memory lane, he couldn't say.

"Hey, boss," Tom called as Coop stepped down from his truck.

They spent the next fifteen minutes touring the area while Coop made note of what had been accomplished and what still needed to be done to get the site up to BarEx, and Oklahoma Corporation Commission standards. A breeze kicked up and a hint of smoke piggybacked on it. November was not the time to burn the alfalfa fields—not that any farmer or rancher would this year, due to the arid conditions. He slowly turned in a circle but didn't see any obvious smoke in the area. He noted both the tractor and the bulldozer that had been used for site prep. He might just leave those in place, at least until the area got some rain. Heavy equipment always came in handy during fire season.

Another vehicle, also bearing the BarEx logo, pulled through the gate. Good. That would be the field geologist. They could get down to business and drill some core samples. Yessir, this was just what he needed—fresh air, a rig site and a job to do. No room for women in his head now. That was his plan, anyway.

Britt stared at the rack of maternity clothes, her mouth turned down in a frown. She was not ready to give up her jeans and Henleys, or her boots. At the same time, the idea of buying jeans two or three sizes larger than normal was so not registering on her cool meter. Eventually, she'd have to admit to her bosses that she wasn't putting on weight, she was pregnant. She hated to do that for myriad reasons, mainly that the powers that be might take her out of the field. Sure, she could relegate her research to the computer lab, relying on others to feed raw data to her to analyze, but that wasn't how she wanted to do things. The way she looked at it, as long as her ob-gyn cleared her for duty, she should be able to do what she loved—chase storms and other weather phenomena.

Before she could convince herself to try on a pair of mom jeans, her phone trilled with the station's alert. She opened her text program and read the information. A small fire had cropped up southwest of Oklahoma City. Winds were out of the south but a weather front caused by an area of high pressure was due to sweep through the state in a matter of hours, bringing with it high winds and low humidity. Given the overgrowth from the wet spring, any fire had the potential to escalate into a disaster.

She hung the jeans back on the rack, and with her phone to her ear, headed for the parking lot. "This is Britt," she said when her call was answered.

"National Weather Service just issued a red flag fire warning for western Oklahoma. I've got crews up near Woodward where a couple of fires are flaring. Can you cover the one southwest of us? It's nothing yet but the potential is there."

"Sure. Where's Leo?"

"He's here at the station. Swing by to pick him up then head toward Chickasha."

"I'll be there in twenty."

Thirty minutes later, she was headed southwest on the H. E. Bailey Turnpike. Leo, settled into the passenger seat, fiddled with the onboard cameras and instruments that would take weather measurements. Neither of them talked. Once Leo was satisfied with all the electronics, he tested communication channels with the station. They were a go if anything newsworthy broke. The horizon in front of them looked clear. The sky to the north showed a thin line of high cirrus clouds, the only sign the dry front was colliding with the hot, humid air. Thunderstorms would be preferable to low humidity even if it meant a chance of lightning.

She'd covered storms of every ilk, a few earthquakes, floods, but wildfires? Fires scared the bejeebers out of her. Once a fire got started, it could create its own weather system, if it was big enough. She'd seen "firenadoes" and other phenomena, including pyrocumulus clouds created when what were normally cute, puffy cumulus clouds turned into Hulk clouds generated by the hot air and smoke from wildfires. They formed when a wildfire burned so hot, it generated an updraft. There was nothing cute or puffy about those suckers. They could literally rain fire and lightning down.

Leo spotted the haze first—a line of dark smoke stretching across the top of a hill. She got off the turnpike at the first available exit and headed toward it.

"You know what they say, where there's smoke—"

She took her eyes off the road just long enough to shoot him a withering glare. "Don't even," she threatened.

"Ah, c'mon, Britt. You know it begs to be said. In fact, I'll buy you a steak dinner at Cattleman's if you say it on air."

"No."

"Chicken."

"Poultry has nothing to do with it. I like my job and prefer to keep it."

"You're totally gonna say it."

"No, I'm not."

"Totally are." He snickered. "And if you don't, you know Dave will."

"Dave's the head meteorologist. He can say whatever he wants."

"Don't you want to move up the food chain?"

She pressed the brake to slow the truck for a stop sign and turned to stare at her partner as they rolled to a stop. "Are you kidding me? Why in the world would you think I'd want to be stuck in the newsroom?"

"Um…because it's a real job?"

"I have a real job."

"Storm chasing is not a real job. Not unless you do it for the Weather Channel. Or one of the universities. Or the government."

She rolled her eyes and moved through the intersection. "I'm also an adjunct professor."

"Oh, and *that's* a real job? No tenure, lower division classes, no teaching assistant."

The road dipped toward a creek bed and they rattled over a one-lane wooden bridge. Topping out on the next hill, Britt hit the brakes. The truck slid to a grinding halt on the red dirt road. Pastures dotted with cedar trees spread out before them. Dry cedar went up like Roman candles when fire hit. To see so many trees scattered across the prairie was a scary sight. Cattle grazed restlessly in a field. Beyond them, to the east, she could just make out the top of a drilling rig—the only part not hidden by another hill. To the west, the voracious fire marched northward, gobbling up the prairie, leaving mounds of smoldering buffalo grass and flaming cedar trees in its wake.

Britt threw the truck into Park, opened her laptop, and started calibrating instruments and analyzing data, all while keeping one eye on the clouds scudding inexorably their way. She grabbed her cell phone and called into the station. The news was not good—not for the rancher who owned that herd of cattle, and not for the crew on the oil rig. She used the running board of her truck as a lookout post, scanning the area for a house. The nearest place that looked inhabited was at least five miles away. In this part of Oklahoma, that wasn't unusual. This was farm and ranch country. If push came to shove—

The scanner and her and Leo's phones all went off. She answered the call while listening to the scanner—a radio call dispatching several fire departments to the grass fire.

"You got Britt," she said into her cell.

"And you got Ria. Dave's coming in and will be looking for live updates. Your GPS puts you near the Grady County fire. Have you got a shot? We'll take you first."

"I can be set up in a few. Will you keep me posted on the front's ETA?"

"For my BFF? Of course I will." Britt could hear the laughter in Ria's voice.

"Whatever. I've got cattle and a drilling rig that might be in the path if the fire changes directions."

"Got ya covered, babe. I'll put you on the Gentner when Dave's ready to go live."

Continuing to call the COMEX communications system a Gentner, the name for an outdated setup, was a station-wide inside joke from the old days.

"I'll go find us a vantage point so the viewers have something to look at."

Ten minutes and a change of position later, she was on-air reporting on the growing grass fire that Leo filmed. The fire was headed away from the cattle and the rig. There were no structures in its immediate path. So long as the strong winds remained blowing from the south, the rancher would lose grazing land but that was all. Sure beat the alternative.

Then Britt sensed the wind shift from south to west. This was bad. A straight front causing a quick directional change wouldn't be a big deal, simply pushing the flames back on the area that had already been burned. But this slow transition was bad. Very bad. The outer edge of the fire had fresh fuel as the wind shifted, spreading it even wider and in a new direction. She leaned across the seat toward the passenger window. "Leo!"

The door opened and the big man climbed in. "Go!"

She didn't wait for him to buckle up. She gunned the truck's engine and they took off down the bumpy road at a speed that wasn't safe under the conditions. She braked, skidding as she jerked the steering wheel to guide the vehicle past the gate leading to the drilling rig. A variety of work trucks and equipment was parked in a graveled area adjoining the rig. She recognized the large white pickup with the now-familiar Barron Exploration logo on the doors. She and Leo jumped out of her vehicle. The tall figure jogging down the metal steps from the drilling rig floor came as no surprise, but his appearance held a heaping helping of annoyance.

"Why me!"

Eight

As Britt tumbled out of her vehicle, Cooper caught what she said. The inflection in her voice indicated both a question and an exclamation, which pretty much summed up the way he felt. He glanced at the large Black man who clambered out of the passenger side. Part of his brain recognized the former football player, but the majority of his focus was on the little spitfire lifting her chin in an attempt to face him down.

"Wha—" The man clipped off what he was about to say as Cooper strode up, stopping in front of Britt.

Hands fisted on his hips, he let his eyes slide up and down her body. She was every bit as sexy as he'd tried to forget. The darn woman haunted his dreams. "Private property, Girl Wonder."

"Won't be any property at all in about ten minutes

unless the wind changes." She jabbed a thumb over her shoulder.

He squinted into the sun and realized what had been smudges of smoke on the horizon were now a solid line of roiling black.

"The wind shifted but not all the way. That fire is headed here. You need to evacuate."

Evacuate? He glanced around. The rig was brand-new, a ten-million-dollar investment. He wouldn't lose it without a fight. "We're set up for fire suppression."

"Don't be stupid, Cooper," she argued.

"I'm not stupid, Britt. Get the hell out while you can. We both know what can happen. We have a fire break and the retention pond is full. I have pumps and hoses and a bulldozer to clear more brush if necessary."

That's when he heard the lowing of the cattle. A small herd was bunching up against the metal fence they'd used to supplement the barbed wire fencing used by the rancher whose land they'd leased for the well. He turned on his heel and took off for the rig where the crew had gathered. He issued orders. A few who claimed prior experience with cattle ran for the fence. The rest split up, some going to move vehicles, the rest to set up the pumps and roll out fire hoses. Cooper headed to the bulldozer.

He climbed into the cab and fired up the diesel engine. Black smoke sputtered from the vertical exhaust pipe as the motor coughed several times before it caught and ran smoothly. As he drove the rumbling machine past Britt's vehicle, he yelled, "Get out, Britt."

The fool woman didn't. She gave her cameraman a

shooing motion with one hand while she jumped into the driver's seat and moved her truck to set up in a slightly safer spot. Idiot woman. Bad enough he had to keep the crew safe but now Britt and…Leo. Leo Blevins. He finally put a name to the face.

He shoved them out of his mind and concentrated on doing what he could to keep them all alive. Chances of a rural fire district crew getting to them were between slim and none. It was up to him, and once they were all safe? He and the Girl Wonder were going to have a serious knock-down drag-out about her tendency to risk her life. The old joke "we have to stop meeting like this" wasn't funny anymore.

Britt watched the big yellow bulldozer knock down a section of the metal rail fence. The cattle weren't frightened at all by the yellow monster belching black smoke. They poured through the gap like some scene from an old Western movie. Four men from the derrick crew waved their arms and more or less herded the cattle toward the large artificial pond. It was filled to the brim with water and she suddenly figured out what the men were doing. If the fire came through the site, they'd drive the cattle into the pond and then jump in themselves. Not ideal but that plan definitely beat the alternative.

Coop was through the gap in the fence now and using the dozer's bucket to scrape up the prairie grass and other vegetation in swaths the length of the site. Back and forth he went as the flames licked ever closer. Leo filmed everything as Britt spoke to Dave, who had their scene live on air. The smoke was getting thicker, and she fought the urge to cough with every inhalation. For a quick moment, she worried about any health affects the bad air might have on her baby, but she had a job to do.

A wall of flames roared no more than ten feet away from the dozer when Cooper turned the machine and headed back through the fence gap. He drove straight to her truck, killed the engine and jumped down. Without so much as a word, he grabbed her around the waist, hoisted her up and ran to the pond, Leo keeping pace.

The crew gathered at the edge of the pond. The cattle had already been herded into the water and the humans were just waiting to see what happened next. There was a lot of dirt and gravel between them and the fire and the hose crews had wet down all the vehicles, the fuel tanks and the rig itself.

"Why didn't you get out of here?" Cooper growled. He actually growled at her, his voice low and rough, and the tone sent a frisson of sexual heat through her. She really needed to have a heart-to-heart with her libido and adrenal gland. Getting turned on in the face of danger was so not cool on so many levels she couldn't count them.

"My job," she managed to answer.

His eyes narrowed on her as his lip curled and he looked away to mouth something probably profane without speaking it out loud. His hand squeezed her hip, and that's when she realized he hadn't turned her loose, only set her on her feet.

Heat and smoke blasted them as a gust of wind hit. The fire was now large enough to generate its own mini-weather front. A fire tornado danced along the leading edge as they were seared again by hot air. The men all had their T-shirts pulled up over their noses and faces. Britt used her arm to cover hers. *Note to self,* she thought. *Start wearing a T-shirt.* Leo had his own T-shirt pulled up over his mouth but his eye remained glued to the eyepiece of his camera.

Her phone kept ringing but she was too mesmerized by the fire coming inexorably closer to answer it. She jumped when water hit them. Two guys remained on one of the fire hoses hooked up to a pump in the pond. They were spraying down people as well as vehicles now. It hurt to breathe, even using her arm as a filter against the smoke. The air was hot and she felt like a steak on a grill, despite the impromptu shower. Another blast of scorching heat hit them. A couple of the crew hit the pond. Almost ready to join them, she didn't get the chance to make the decision on her own.

Cooper reacted out of instinct. He pushed Britt into the water at the same time he ordered the crew in. He was about to shove Leo in, camera and all, when the big man set the camera down, lens still facing the fire, and then took a running leap into the water, hitting the surface with a belly flop. Coop was right behind him. Britt had just struggled to her feet and was as spitting mad as a wet cat. He didn't give her a chance to chew him out. He grabbed her and took her down with him. He'd heard her gasp as they went under and he really hoped she'd taken a deep breath before they did. Of course, he could always give her mouth-to-mouth. He smiled and wanted to laugh despite the gravity of their situation. For a man who was not an adrenaline junkie, hanging around with Britt was becoming not only hazardous to his health and welfare but somewhat addictive too.

When she thrashed against him, he loosened his hold just enough so their faces could surface. Then he raised his head and looked around. Everyone else slowly surfaced as well. The wind had shifted to the north at the very last minute. They were safe.

The cattle headed to shore, as did the crew. Leo grabbed his camera, checked it and grinned. "That was too freaking close, boys and girl."

"You can say that again," one of the crew muttered.

Leo opened his mouth and Britt cut him off. "Don't be that guy," she cautioned. She pulled her phone out of her hip pocket and grimaced. "Maybe a blow dryer and a week in a bag of rice will revive it. If not, I'll just mortgage my life savings to buy a waterproof phone."

Cooper pulled his waterproof phone from his pocket and handed it to her. "Here, feel free to use mine." She was reaching for it when her phone actually rang.

"It's a miracle," she breathed and answered, "We're still breathing, Ria."

The men wandered off to check the rig and their vehicles. The cattle stood bunched together, a little shell-shocked, which was precisely how Coop felt. They eventually wandered off to the side where there'd been no fire and nibbled any grass they could reach through the fence.

A few of the trucks and the bulldozer had spots where the paint had bubbled from the heat. The rig itself was fine, as were the fuel tanks. He checked Britt's truck while she talked to the TV station. It had been parked closest to the retention pond and appeared to be fine. Sirens sounded in the distance and within minutes, a line of fire engines and brush pumpers passed by on the road, lights and sirens going. Several vehicles pulled in, including a chief.

Coop walked over to talk to the man in charge of the fire team.

"Y'all got lucky," the man called as he approached.

"For sure."

The firefighter driving the chief looked around. "Saved the cattle too."

"Yup."

"Got enough water in the pond that we can use some to fill our tankers?"

"Absolutely."

"And the bulldozer?"

"You got that too if needed. Whatever we can do to help."

"Appreciate it. Sorry we didn't get here in time to keep you from getting all wet."

Coop twisted the hem of his polo to wring out the excess water. "Warm day. Cold water. Nice break."

The chief laughed. "Y'all take any damage?"

"Not to speak of. I make safety a priority."

"Smart man."

"I try to be."

The older man nodded. "I roger that. Appreciate the assistance. And if you don't mind, I'd like to set up my command post and R and R area here. The Red Cross isn't too far behind us."

"No problem. Feel free to draft my crew to help you set up."

Cooper's phone rang and he checked the caller ID. His office. "I need to take this, Chief." The man waved him off, speaking into a radio as Coop turned his back and answered just as Britt had. "We're still breathing."

"Good to know." Cord's voice sounded amused. "But we can see that. Y'all are live on the TV. Wanna explain why Britt's there and you're soaking wet?"

"We decided to have a pool party."

Cord was laughing out loud now. "No skinny-dipping?"

"Dude, the only female here is Britt and I'd hate to have to shoot our crew because they saw her naked. They're a good crew and I don't want to train another."

Still chuckling, Cord asked if Cooper needed anything. "Nope. We're good to go. Fire chief wants to use the site as his command post. Red Cross is gonna set up an R and R area. I've loaned them the crew to help set up."

"What are you gonna do?"

"Drive the bulldozer if they need it."

"Sounds like fun. Stay safe out there, cuz."

"Absolutely, boss."

"And, Cooper? All kidding aside, I'm glad you're okay and thanks for making me see the point of all the extra work. They're a good crew and I damn sure didn't want to tell their families that they weren't coming home."

"Just doin' my job, Cord."

"Well, nobody does it better."

They cleared the call simultaneously, Cooper feeling a little embarrassed. Ever since their accident, Cord had been as safety conscious as Coop. Still, it felt good to know his persnickety tendencies were appreciated. He tucked his phone away and headed toward the knot of official vehicles.

Two of the firefighters leaned against their brush pumper, watching Britt. He didn't like the glint in their eyes, or the speculative looks on their faces. As he got closer, he heard one say, "Pretty little storm chaser is all wet."

"Indeed she is," the second one agreed.

Cooper was not at all pleased they were discussing her. Britt was going to be his. Sooner or later. He glanced over at her. She wore a dark shirt so even though it was plastered to her body, it didn't reveal much. Except it was plastered to her body and Coop had been fantasizing about her body for months now and he darn sure didn't remember her breasts being that large nor the roundness of her belly. He blinked. And everything inside him went cold.

Nine

Britt continued to give spot reports until one of the regular reporters showed up to take over. In between conversations with the station and on-air time, she watched Cooper. The few times she caught him looking at her, she couldn't decipher his expression. He looked angry but confused, with a side of narrow-eyed speculation, almost like she was some sort of criminal. What had she done wrong? Her brain jumped on its hamster wheel and she caught a glimpse of her reflection in the tinted window of her truck.

Her clothes were wet, though drying. Except her cotton Henley was plastered to her body. *Really* plastered. Her added curves were visible to anyone who looked. And Cooper had been looking. A lot. She reminded her lungs to work. This was bad. If he guessed before she told him… Or maybe he'd just think that she was seeing someone else. Yes. That was the ticket. If he thought she had a boyfriend, then he would never think he was the father and she wouldn't have to tell him, except… she'd be lying. And while she might be a lot of things, a liar was not one of them. She had to tell him. But not here and definitely not now.

A gust of wind blew through and it chilled her. Goose bumps rose on her arms and she shivered. She searched the back seat of her truck and found the go bag she'd stuffed in there earlier in the fall. Digging through it, she found dry jeans, a shirt and more important, underwear. All she had to do now was find a place to change. Straightening, she surveyed the rig site. A metal building that looked like some sort of office sat next to the rig. If she was lucky, it might have indoor plumbing too.

Cooper was the last person she wanted to talk to so she watched to see which of the BarEx crew she should ask. An older man seemed to be giving instructions so she waited to approach him until Cooper was busy with the fire chief.

"Um, hi," she said to the man's back. He turned around and smiled.

"What can I do you for, darlin'?"

"Is that building like an office or something?"

"Or something. Whatcha need?"

"A place to change clothes and maybe use the…uh… facilities?"

He managed not to smile but she caught the twinkle in his eyes. "Door's open, and there's a lock on it. Help yourself."

She flashed him a smile of thanks and jogged over. She checked Cooper's location to make sure he wasn't looking at her. He was still busy with the chief so she ducked inside and locked the door.

Britt ran into a problem when she tried to button and zip up the jeans. She muttered several four-letter words before stretching out with her back on the desk and just managed to get the darn things fastened. She had to roll off the desk because she couldn't sit up while breathing and at that point in time, breathing was of utmost importance. The jeans were uncomfortable and she considered popping both the button and the zipper and just keeping her shirttails out to cover up. Except as sure as she did that, someone would notice. Like Cooper. That man didn't miss a trick.

After a few moments, she got her breath back and decided she'd be fine so long as she didn't have to sit down. Sitting and breathing would be completely incompatible. She shouldn't have put off her shopping trip. And it was time to address the proverbial elephant in the room. She had to tell Cooper, the sooner the better.

Cooper covertly watched Britt. He didn't want to think what he was thinking. The odds were hardly favorable but given the file on Chance's desk concerning Susan Maddox's paternity accusation and the court-ordered DNA tests, he couldn't keep his thoughts from going there. Maybe she'd just put on weight. That was entirely possible. It wasn't like she was a true on-air personality who had some sort of contract clause that decreed she wear a size five or something. And she definitely hadn't been built like a runway model last August. But now? Not that he didn't appreciate the curves. He definitely did, yet something was different about her.

It took some maneuvering before he stood next to Leo. He opened the conversation with what he considered safe territory. "Tackle, right?"

"Nope. Tackle, left."

He laughed. "Good one. I thought I recognized you."

"Not many do anymore."

"How long have you been on TV?"

It was the cameraman's turn to laugh. "Not exactly *on* the tube. I was a communications major. Thought I'd do sportscasting if I couldn't go pro. Then I heard my voice." He let out a booming laugh. "Yeah…no. Not to mention I hate wearing a tie. So I grabbed a camera."

"You been with Britt long?"

A bushy black eyebrow rose. "A while."

Cooper considered his next question carefully but Leo beat him to it. "If you're interested, I can save you the trouble. She'll shut you down like she does every other guy. That little gal hasn't gone on a date in the two years I've known her."

Which was a good news/bad news situation as far as Coop was concerned. Because she'd been with him. Several times. Two and two kept coming up four and he got a sinking feeling in the pit of his stomach. "Yeah… well. I'll just have to change her mind about that."

Britt stared out the windshield. This was so not a good idea. Why she'd ever agreed to meet Cooper for a late dinner was beyond her. She was tired and her hair still smelled faintly of smoke. Today's fire had been exhausting to cover.

"You're going to regret this," she muttered. She did not want to confide in him. Not that she wouldn't. The man had a right to know. She didn't see his truck in the Mexican restaurant's parking lot. Wondering why he'd suggested this place, she continued to just sit there. She'd wanted to eat here for ages but never had. Now, her stomach was turning somersaults and she wasn't sure she'd be able to sample the food.

She'd dreaded this moment from the instant that stupid pregnancy test showed a plus sign. Britt didn't have to wonder who the father was. There'd been only one. She snorted and rolled her eyes at her reflection in the rearview mirror. Wasn't that the tag line to some old TV show about immortal highlanders?

Someone tapped on her window. Britt squealed and recoiled. Then she recognized Cooper's face peering in at her.

"You okay, Girl Wonder?"

"I'm fine." Okay, that came out snippier than it should have, but he had startled her. "Just waiting on you to get here."

"I've been here."

She looked around the parking lot again. "Where's your truck?"

"At home. I brought my Expedition."

Well, crud. Of course he'd have more than one vehicle. "If you have an Expedition, why did you drive your truck to the gala?"

"Company branding."

"What?"

"Are you getting out or what? We can talk inside. I have a cold drink and hot queso in there waiting."

"Or what," she muttered under her breath, reluctant to open the door and get out. Still, it was time.

Inside the restaurant, he held her chair. She sank into it, gave her drink order to the waitress, and eyed the basket of tortilla chips, salsa, queso and relish. Her stomach rumbled. Good to know that she could eat. She reached for the chips and when the waitress returned with her iced tea, Britt ordered hot tortillas—a mix of corn and flour.

As she plowed through the chips, then the tortillas, she framed what she was going to say in her mind. Cooper sat across from her, watching with an amused look and occasionally getting brave enough to snatch a chip. Once their food arrived, she debated whether to wait until after dinner. Okay, until after she had a sopapilla. Those little pillows of fried bread drenched in honey were a favorite dessert. Too bad Cooper beat her to the punch.

"When are you due?"

She choked on the bite of enchilada she'd just put in her mouth, barely managing to chew, swallow and grab a gulp of tea before staring at him, eyes wide. She stalled, hoping she'd heard wrong. "Beg pardon?"

"When's your due date?"

Yeah. She'd heard him correctly. She took another sip then dabbed at her lips with her napkin before meeting his gaze. "First week in June." She watched him make the calculations in his head and decided to distract him. "How did you know I'm pregnant?"

Okay, it was fairly obvious—loose clothing, noticeable baby bump that was more like a small hill than a bump. He studied her, all traces of amusement gone.

"Who's the father?"

She glanced around the restaurant. No one was seated nearby to overhear her. That excuse to avoid the topic wasn't available. She lifted a shoulder in a negligent shrug as she lifted her chin in stubborn pride. "You."

"What do you want?"

Now that surprised her. No argument. No denial. No pleading. Just direct and to the point. Maybe this wouldn't be so bad after all. "Nothing."

That made him blink. He leaned his elbows on the table, framing his plate of beef fajitas. "Nothing?"

"You got it. I don't want your money or anything else from you." She leaned forward and dropped her voice conspiratorially. "I'm guessing the condom broke or something. Since you're the one who can't keep your little cowboy wrangled in your jeans, you should check the best-if-used-by dates on those things."

Britt hoped that by going on the offensive, she'd put Cooper off. She couldn't decipher his expression, and deep down, she wanted to poke at him to get a response. Some other woman might be having his baby. She definitely was. And his lack of reaction bothered her. A lot. He continued to watch her and she made a mental note never to play strip poker with the guy.

"I'm a big girl. I knew what I was doing and accept

the responsibility." She put down her fork and leaned back. "I'm not trying to trap you, Cooper. We had fun together. We got caught. I'm dealing with it."

He continued to stare and she wondered what was going through his head.

"Sounds like you have it all figured out." His voice sounded flat. "And since you have, I'm curious as to why you decided to involve me at all."

Did he really just say that to her? "Because you're the father! You have a right to know." She rubbed at her forehead, hoping to stave off the headache forming behind her eyes. "Look. Bad timing, given that other situation."

"That *other* situation? You mean the woman trying to scam me out of child support for a baby that isn't mine?"

"So *you* say."

"I do say. And the DNA test will prove it. In the meantime, I have a solution to *this* situation."

The next words out of his mouth sent her into a tailspin.

"We'll get married."

She almost choked again. "No!" Now she leaned on the table and they were almost nose-to-nose. "You want to pay child support? Awesome. But I am not marrying you just because I'm pregnant."

"Why not?"

"What do you mean why not? Because…just…no. I don't love you." *But you could.* She shushed that voice in her head, all the while wondering why that was her first argument. "I barely know you. Granted, the sex is off the charts but that is not a good basis for a marriage."

He broke first—sort of. He didn't lose her gaze as he seemed to relax, leaning back into his chair. He raised a rolled tortilla filled with fajita meat and grilled onions and peppers to his mouth. Biting it, he continued to hold her eyes as he chewed, then swallowed. "Why didn't you do something about it when you found out?"

It was her turn to blink, surprised. Several things came to mind but it was the truth that tumbled out, much to her chagrin. "Because it's your baby too." She closed her eyes and rubbed her temple. "What I mean is, I wouldn't have done something like that without contacting you first. Granted most men would totally agree to the procedure—"

"I wouldn't have."

She slowly closed her mouth. He kept talking.

"I still want to marry you."

"I'm still confused. That accuser at the gala—"

"Is lying through his teeth. I'd never seen his sister before she arrived at my cousin's office with her brother and their attorney. Do you have any idea how many paternity suits my family gets hit with?"

"How do you know I'm not lying?"

"Because I know. I was there. I'm the one who discovered that the condom broke but by the time I got out of the bathroom, you'd already disappeared. Again. I assumed you were on some form of birth control. Guess you weren't."

She blushed, and slid her gaze away from his for a long moment. "I was busy and I forgot when I was due for my shot. I wasn't dating anyone so it wasn't a big deal. You used condoms. And then..." She made an exploding gesture with her fingers. "My world sort of blew up. By the time I remembered about the Depo shot, it was too late. I was throwing up and buying a pregnancy test."

"Were you ever going to tell me?" He sounded… hurt. That surprised her.

"Yeah. Eventually. I don't want you to feel obligated, Cooper."

"Yeah, you don't get it. I *am* obligated. You say you want to take responsibility. Well, guess what, Girl Wonder. It took both of us to make that baby." His lips curved up into a smile that would melt the panties off any woman who saw it. "As you say, the chemistry between us is exceptional. So, we'll get married and I'll take care of you and the baby."

"No."

"Why are you being so stubborn about this? Any other woman would be jumping at the chance."

"I'm not any other woman. I'm me."

Now it was his turn to sigh, close his eyes and rub his temple. When he looked at her again, his expression caused her heart to skip a beat. "If you won't marry me, I want joint custody."

Ten

Cooper didn't smirk at the look of surprised confusion on Britt's face. He'd remained very calm. He had to, given the evidence. The timing was right. The condom had broken. And, at least according to Leo, Britt didn't date or fool around. Except she had with him. He thought back to that night. She'd come on hot and heavy. The sex had been her idea. But then she'd disappeared the next morning. He didn't get the sense she was scamming him, though a guy could never be too careful.

"Are you kidding me?" she finally asked.

"Nope." He wasn't kidding. If the DNA test proved the kid was his, he'd support the child monetarily, but also emotionally. No way he'd go for anything besides joint custody. Of course, that would give him lots of reasons to hang around Britt. He wouldn't have been at all unhappy if she'd agreed to marry him. He was already half in love with her, crazy as that seemed. He wasn't the only brother who'd been hit by the Curse of the Tate Men. He always capitalized the phrase like it was a title or was important. Denver, his dad, sat each of his brothers down in their early teens for the birds and the bees talk, and he finished with two admonitions—always wear a condom and beware of the Curse of the Tate Men.

"Tate men," Denver Tate had said in that booming voice of his, "are cursed to love only one woman and to love her hard and forever. You'll know when the right one comes along. Don't be settlin' for less, boy. You hear me?"

As sure as his mother wore pearls, he'd been cursed.

And frankly, it didn't feel too bad. Britt was funny, intelligent, gorgeous, stubborn. Well, okay. Maybe that last one should go in the negative column but at least things would never get boring. She reminded him of his mother just a little bit, not that he would ever mention that to either woman. He might be dumb but he wasn't stupid.

"Why in the world would a man like you want to share joint custody of a child?"

"A man like me?" He didn't mean for his voice to sound quite as threatening as it came out but his tone sure made Britt sit up and take notice. Wide-eyed and pressed back in her chair, she stared at him. "What's that supposed to mean?"

She swallowed hard and he watched her throat work, which stirred up things inside him. Nope, chemistry was never a problem between them. When she just continued to stare, he cocked a brow—a dare he knew she couldn't resist.

"Well, you know."

"No, I don't know. That's why I asked."

"You're rich."

"I also work for a living."

"You're single."

"I offered to marry you."

"What do you know about kids?"

"I have nieces and nephews." Well, *a* niece and *a* nephew that were Tates. There were more if he included the Barron cousins.

"Why would you want to tie yourself down?"

"Why would you?"

Her mouth opened. Closed. Opened. Closed. Forehead furrowed, she studied him. "Why would you even ask that?"

He held up his right index finger. "You work for a living—two jobs. One of which has crazy hours." He added his middle finger. "You're single." He ticked up a third finger. "What do you know about kids?"

Britt did the whole fish out of water imitation again before clamping her mouth shut. "Point to you," she finally admitted. "But you're a guy."

"Glad you noticed."

"Gah." She rolled her eyes. "You know what I mean. I figured a man like you would be glad to be absolved of responsibility."

"Well, I'm not. In fact, I'm kinda offended you'd think that."

That got a reaction. She rocked back, tucking her chin as she frowned. "I don't know what to say to that."

"Considering that you keep insulting me, maybe you should only open your mouth to eat." He didn't hide the smile sliding across his face as he considered other things he'd like her mouth to do. He focused on his own meal while watching her out of his peripheral vision. He'd call Chance once he and Britt were finished to fill him in on current events and to get some safeguards set up, just in case Britt continued to balk.

And didn't that make him all cool, calm and collected. He should be angry at the most, dubious and suspicious at the least. Except she hadn't shown up on his doorstep demanding things. In fact, Britt had done her best to avoid him. Then she refused his offer of marriage. He still wanted a DNA test but he knew with a certainty that surprised him the child was his.

"When's your next doctor's appointment?"

She very carefully chewed and swallowed the bite she'd just forked into her mouth before responding. "Why?"

"Because I'm going with you."

"Oh no you—"

"Yes. I need to speak to his—"

"Her. My OB is female."

"Good to know. I need to give her staff my insurance and contact information. I should help cover medical expenses. Besides, I want to be there."

Taken aback, she considered his offer. "It's an ultrasound."

"Good."

"Do you even know what that is?"

He leveled her with a cool-eyed look. "Yes. When are you scheduled?"

"Right before Christmas."

"Give me the date, time and place. I'll be there."

Cooper faced the room full of men. Their expressions matched the roles they were there to play. He was not looking forward to breaking the news to his family. They'd be concerned. He also wondered if he should warn Britt. His relatives, especially the Barron wives—or Bee Dubyas for short—could get overwhelming in a hurry.

He needed a cup of coffee before the dam broke. Nikki, ever her omniscient and efficient self, bumped through his office door bearing a tray full of mugs and a large thermal carafe of coffee. She flashed a cheeky grin and in a loud stage whisper said, "My birthday is next month and there's a pair of diamond earrings I've had my eye on. I'll put them on the company card in lieu of a bonus for my years of selfless service."

She deposited the tray on his desk and gave a perky wiggle of her fingers as she exited. Cord watched her leave before he turned to Coop. "She has a company card?"

Cooper stared at him. "Well…yeah. Doesn't Maureen?"

"Well…yeah, but that's different."

He rolled his eyes at his cousin and boss. "Sure it is."

Glancing toward the door, Cord muttered something about the accountants and discussing with his administrative assistant how she used the credit card. Coop laughed. "If Nikki actually followed through every time she threatened to buy diamonds with that card, we'd own stock in Tiffany's."

"Now that joke time is over," Chance interrupted, his lawyer face firmly in place, "we need to talk about this situation with Britt Owens."

"Not a situation, Chance, and *we* aren't doing a thing."

"Cooper," Bridger started.

"Look, I called y'all last night after I forced the issue with Britt. Paternity is not confirmed but it will be. What I need from you, Chance—"

Cash jumped into the conversation. "Chance is right, Cooper. We need to step back and assess things. We've all been here."

"Except me," Bridger said. "I'm the good son."

Cooper nailed him in the head with a wadded-up ball of paper. "You better knock wood, Bridge. I was with Britt. In Beaumont. The times line up." His pronouncement dropped into a well of silence. "I'm pretty sure I'm the father of her baby."

"Dad taught us better, Coop."

"I wore a condom, Bridger. Both times."

"Wait," Cord interrupted. "*Britt* was the one who disappeared on you down there? The one you've been mooning over since you got home in September."

Bridger nodded sagely. "Yup. She would be the one. Mom had it figured out before any of the rest of us but, man…" He shook his head now, looking dubious.

"The timing on her little announcement is all kinds of wrong."

"I've never been with that Susie..." Coop snapped his fingers a couple of times trying to recall her name. "Maddox. Have no clue who she is. And the DNA test will prove I'm not the father of her baby. I'm not in the habit of discussing my sex life with anyone much less you miscreants yet I've admitted that Britt and I were together."

Cord leaned back in his chair. "So if you wore a condom, how can you be so sure the baby is yours?"

"Because the damn thing broke."

Chance put down his coffee mug. "I want you to think very carefully about how you answer this, Cooper." His gaze was so intent, Coop had to clear his throat. Then he nodded, waiting for what Chance would say next. "What exactly do you mean by the condom broke?"

Coop could almost see the air quotes around those last four words. "Because when I took it off, the top had partially separated from the sides. It broke, Chance."

"She could have messed with it. Did she have the chance to get at your wallet?" his ever-helpful boss asked.

"Yeah...about that. I used the one in my wallet the night before."

"So she gave you the condom?" Chance pushed. "She could have poked a hole in the package."

"No!" Coop glared at his cousin. "She didn't touch the thing. I dug it out of the drawer on the bedside table of the company's RV." He felt sheepish and probably looked like it if the expressions on his brothers' and cousins' faces were any indication. "Who knew those things come with an expiration date. It had been in the drawer for…a really long time."

The others exchanged looks and Coop felt like he was fourteen again, getting The Lecture from his dad—the one about girls and condoms and the Curse of the Tate Men.

Coop could still hear his dad's voice, a rich baritone with an edge, a gruff gravelly tone like he smoked two packs a day, though the man had only smoked seven cigars in his entire life. One for each of his sons. He missed his dad so much. A big man who worked with his hands, an old-school rancher who'd given his sons all the right advice. Then he'd died. Sudden cardiac death, the doctor said. He and Tucker had found him in the barn, sitting on a bale of hay, looking like he was taking a nap.

He'd watched Deke fall in love and then Tucker. And told both of them that they weren't being smart to fall so hard and fast. Quin and Noelle completed Deke, just as Zoe and Nash did the same for Tuck. Neither child was a Tate by blood, but they sure were by love. Deke and Quin had adopted Noelle and Tuck had adopted Zoe's little boy. Britt's baby was his. Did he love Britt? He wasn't sure. Was he falling in love with her? Oh, yeah. She wasn't anything he'd ever wanted in a woman but he'd discovered she was everything he wanted.

His phone pinged a reminder and he breathed a little easier. Inquisition over. "Britt's having an ultrasound this morning. I'm not missing it because y'all are doing this intervention thing. I plan to marry her, but just in case, I want papers..." He met Chance's concerned gaze. "Joint custody. If she won't marry me, I want joint custody. Make it happen."

Time to make his exit before his brother and cousins pounced. "I know y'all planned an intervention. I don't need one."

He exited to the sound of stunned silence.

Sitting in the break room at the TV station killing time before her appointment, Britt couldn't quite meet Ria's gaze. She sipped her orange juice, wondering why no one had figured out how to caffeinate juice. Oh, wait. That would be soda pop. But as far as coffee was concerned, her doctor insisted she cut back on the only substance guaranteed to get her through the day.

"Girl, you make me crazy." Ria *tsked*, shaking her head, an indulgent expression on her face. "At least he's stepping up and taking responsibility just on your say-so. That's got to be a first in that family."

She snorted. "Oh, he demanded a DNA test, but he's also convinced that he's the father."

"Which he is. You're my best friend. I can count the number of men you've slept with on one hand. And none of them in at least the last year. Of course he's the father."

Coughing to hide her mutter, Britt said, "Two years."

She'd been such an idiot that first time with Cooper. Seeing Leo—a huge man full of muscles and swagger—felled by a stupid trash can lid had done something to her. Watching the water rise, the wind rip buildings apart, knowing that people were going to die? All of that settled deep in her soul, making her understand how fragile life truly was. And how alone she was. When Cooper opened the door to the BarEx offices, all she'd wanted to do was burrow into his arms and hide. To do something spontaneous and outrageous and not like her. So she had. She'd grabbed life with both hands and propositioned him.

That night had been totally worth it. And then when he'd rescued her and the others that next night? And the morning that followed? Heck yeah, she'd cut and run both times out of fear and a sense of self-preservation. The man was a potent combination of funny and handsome, of brains and muscles, and all the things that made the alarm on her biological clock ring. And when that condom broke? Her sadly neglected ovaries must have gone into overdrive.

"I'm an idiot," she muttered.

"Yes and no. I think you're being smart to take things slow." Ria reached across the table and squeezed her hand. "He's taking care of the bills. That's only right. And he's interested. Good grief, the chemistry between you two is off the charts. Get to know him." She held up her free hand, cutting off Britt's intended retort. "I'm aware he asked you to marry him, and you think it's out of some antiquated sense of duty. Maybe it is but let me tell you, Miz Britt, men like that are few and far between. Date. Let him take care of things. Get. To. Know. Him. Who knows? That chemistry might just turn into the real deal."

And that was precisely what scared her the most.

Eleven

Britt walked into her doctor's office and halted mid-step. Cooper stood at the check-in window, one elbow braced casually on the tall counter as he spoke to the receptionist. The woman stared at him raptly, like he was some Olympic god come to earth or something. Okay, he did look utterly awesome in those pressed jeans, boots, a shirt as blue as his eyes, and the leather jacket.

Everything went into slow motion as he turned his head to look at Britt, a smile teasing those so-kissable lips of his, the fluorescent lights catching in his eyes so that they twinkled. He checked her out, from head to toe, and heat washed over her.

Then she saw red as the totally skinny and primped woman behind the counter slid a card toward Coop and Britt read her lips. “Here’s my number. Call me anytime.”

Cooper ignored the woman and her card. Instead, he stalked across the office toward Britt. She forced air into her lungs. Who knew breathing was so hard to do? The red faded from her vision, but she noticed the gaze of every female in the place, from sixteen to sixty, was trained on him. The testosterone haze he exuded was so potent, she was pretty sure he could get a girl pregnant just by looking at her. Of course, she knew all about that, didn’t she?

“Howdy, Girl Wonder.”

No, her panties were *not* going to disappear just from the sound of his voice or the heat in his eyes. *Nope. Not happening.* Nor would she swoon because if she did, he’d catch her, and she’d be a goner if he touched her.

“Fancy meeting you here, Hero Boy.”

“I keep tellin’ you—”

“Yeah, yeah. You’re not a boy. And I’m not a girl. I need to get checked in.”

After she signed in, he led her to a couch set back in the far corner of the waiting room. They didn’t have time to sit before her name was called.

Britt turned to go, stopping when Coop touched her arm. “I’d really…” He cleared his throat and she saw raw emotion shine through his eyes for a moment. “If you don’t mind, I’d like to go back with you.”

Her first instinct was to say, “No way.” But she couldn’t resist the plea in his eyes. “Okay.”

The sonographer was all smiles as she walked them back to a fairly large room with an exam table, a couch and a comfy chair. A utilitarian cart filled with all sorts of electronic gear was parked next to the exam table. A giant-screen TV was mounted to the opposite wall.

"You can pull the chair over close to our little momma, if you want, Dad."

Britt gritted her teeth. Why did so many health care workers get all honey-sweet and cutesy? Their demeanor irritated the snot out of her on a good day and today? Today was so not a good day. She woke up with indigestion, a frantic need to pee and a headache. Then she'd had to cover a class for another adjunct professor who'd decided to take off for Christmas early, which meant an unplanned trip to the campus in Norman. And her truck was sitting on empty so she had to stop and get gas. The automatic shutoff on the hose didn't click off when her tank was full, gasoline spilled on her shoes and she'd gotten into a shouting match with the convenience store clerk over the mess.

And Cooper had been waiting for her all spit and polished and handsome, getting flirted with by a woman who looked perfect and—

"Shhh, darlin'."

She blinked at him. "What?"

"You're growling. Here. I'll help you up."

The next thing she knew, his hands were on her sides and he lifted her easily to sit on the table. While the tech got her prepped, Coop dragged the chair over, sat down and took her hand. Then the tech squirted cold, gushy gel on her bared belly. The sonographer pressed the wand against her skin then made some adjustments to the machine. Moments later, a picture popped up on the big screen.

For several minutes, the tech moved the wand, keeping up a running commentary. The baby was on track for its age. And it had a cute butt, which was the only recognizable body part she could see.

"Your little one is being shy. Let me move over here to see if we can get a look at its face."

The image on the screen blinked off and when it came back on, the silence in the room was as thick as red clay. Two heads. Were those arms? Britt quickly counted. Four. And four legs. The sonographer squealed like a cheerleader.

"Twins!"

Britt glanced at the walking definition of testosterone and had one thought. Of course, he'd produce twins. Heck, it wouldn't matter if the condom didn't break or if she'd been current on her Depo shot. Her eggs never had a chance against his champion swimmers. She stared at him while his eyes remained glued to the TV.

She heard some clicks and the wand moved again, followed by more clicks. "I'll print out two copies of all the pictures," the sonographer said. "They look so cute. Too bad we can't tell their sex."

She did *not* want to think about sex of any sort. That's what got her into this in the first place.

Thirty minutes later, the goop had been cleaned off her belly, they each had a set of the ultrasound pictures, and she was sitting in Coop's truck, too stunned to argue when he guided her to it in the parking lot. He settled into the driver's seat, started the truck and punched the buttons for the heater. That's when she realized she was shivering.

"I'm not cold."

"I know."

"Twins."

"Yeah, I know."

Did he sound gleeful? She turned to look at him. He was staring straight ahead but the grin on his face crinkled his cheeks and eyes—at least the ones on the right side. He shifted in the seat so he could look at her.

"Marry me, Britt."

"No."

"Why not?"

"For all the same reasons I've given you before."

"Then move in with me?"

"Wha—? Why?"

"So I can take care of you."

"I don't need anyone to take care of me."

"Darlin', we all need someone to take care of us."

She refused to acknowledge that bit of logic. He remained silent for a few minutes and the shivers stopped as the truck warmed.

"Then spend Christmas with me."

"No." Okay, that was a knee-jerk reaction but she didn't want anything to do with him at the moment, especially Christmas, because she couldn't trust herself.

"Why not?"

"I have plans." She didn't, but she'd make some. Today. And he didn't need to know.

"I want to introduce you to my family."

"No."

"Britt." He was wheedling. And it was working. She didn't have family. Not anymore.

"New Year's then."

"I have plans."

Cooper went stiff, his voice barely above a growl when he asked, "Do you have a date?"

Was he jealous? Britt mentally rolled her eyes. What did he have to be jealous of? Not that she *did* have a date.

Before she could confirm or deny, he added, "I'm sure I don't need to remind you that you're having my babies."

Jerk. She swiveled to face him. "Like I could forget? You're not the one with the swollen feet and ankles, the acid reflux, and the obsessive need to know the location of every public restroom between here and there. Why do you even care, Cooper? I've given you the perfect escape. Most men would thank me and disappear so fast they'd leave skid marks. But you? Noooo. Not you. You have to stick your nose in with your demands and your sense of duty and honor and responsibility. Why can't you just be a big ol' weenie like most—"

Before she could finish her rant, she was in his arms and he was kissing her. *Really* kissing her. Like he was dying of thirst and her mouth was the sweetest water in the world. She knew the feeling and wow, was she thirsty for him too.

She was in so much trouble. She pushed away from him and seeing the satisfied smirk on his face, she wanted to clobber him with a two-by-four. Since she didn't have one handy, she scrambled back into her seat, reaching for the door handle. "Go away, Cooper Tate. Go far, far away. I don't want to marry you. I'm not moving in with you. In fact, I pretty much hate you at the moment."

She clambered out and clung to the door until she got her balance. Cooper made no move to get out. She glowered up at him. "I don't need a husband *or* a boyfriend. Just stay away from me."

"I'll pick you up for dinner."

She slammed the door so hard the whole truck rocked. She could still hear his laughter as she climbed into her own vehicle. She managed to get it started, in gear and backed out of the parking space. The rest of her drive home was a blur until she realized she was parked outside her condo. Then she thunked her head on the steering wheel and ignored the tears.

"Twins." What was she supposed to do now?

Britt stared at the bouquet of flowers—a beautiful Christmas arrangement in a crystal vase. From the weight of it, the thing was real cut glass. She almost hadn't opened the door and was now wishing she hadn't. The delivery driver thrust the flowers into her hands and boogied back down the sidewalk before she could react. She cautiously set the vase on her kitchen counter. A card was tucked into the extravagant green and red plaid bow.

Her fingers shook slightly as she freed the envelope, opened it, and withdrew the card. The handwriting was bold. Firm. And she recognized the signature. *Merry Christmas. I'll pick you up at 7:00 for dinner.*

Dress casual. Cooper. Her heart did a little giddy-up and she swallowed around the lump of anticipation in her throat. No. Just…no. He was wearing her down. Flowers. Lunches delivered from her favorite restaurants. And flowers. Not every day. But often enough. And deep down, what woman didn't appreciate flowers? Food and flowers were one path to her heart. His calls and concern and always asking if there was something he could do to help derailed her resolve.

The man was nothing if not persistent.

She'd go to dinner. And she'd tell him again, when he asked, that she would not marry him. Except more and more often, daydreams crept in. She'd be staring at a screen shot of a radar presentation looking for data and zap! Just like that, a thought of what it would be like to be sitting in her own space at his house would hit her. Surely there was room in that place for an office all her own, a spot where she could hang maps and whiteboards on the walls. With a worktable holding printouts and photos. A desk with her computer and a printer. A place that could stay messy—well, it would seem messy to anyone but her. She'd know where everything was. *Her* office where she could decorate it any way she wanted, where she could shut the door and walk away from her research, knowing it would all be in the exact same place the next time she entered. She really didn't want much.

And then there were those daydreams of sleeping in his arms, of the kissing and touching and making love that went with sharing the same bed. Since the night of the November gala, she'd found lots of excuses to take weird detours when she drove to the TV station, all of them designed to keep her away from Cooper's house, but she still ended up driving past it, and straining to catch a glimpse of it. Or the man.

And there she went again, lost in thoughts of the man who'd become the bane of her existence. But if he stopped calling, texting, dropping by—and sending her flowers—she'd miss him.

Cooper leaned back in his chair and pretended his fingers didn't itch to touch Britt. Since they'd first gotten the news she was having twins, he'd managed to con her into going out with him several times. The Christmas arrangement he'd had delivered that day also worked. After picking her up, they'd driven to Othello's in Norman, the iconic Italian restaurant on Campus Corner. Ensconced at a table in a dark corner, he watched her eat, plotting how best to get his way. He wanted to spend Christmas with her. And he wanted her to move in with him. Better if she married him, but just having her under his roof would go a long way in his plan to seduce her into accepting his proposal.

"Stop staring."

"I can't help it."

She blinked up at him, slowly chewing the bite of chicken parmigiana she'd just taken. He tracked the muscles in her throat as she swallowed. "What do you mean? Staring at people while they eat is just plain rude."

"You're beautiful."

She rolled her eyes in an exaggerated manner. "Don't change the subject. And don't you dare say I'm glowing."

He flashed her a half smile at that declaration. "Well, you might be glowing just a little. And you are beautiful. You also look tired. I don't like seeing the dark circles under your eyes." He reached across the table and took her free hand in his. "I want to take care of you, Britt."

She bristled, as he knew she would. "I can take care of myself."

"Of course you can. But you don't have to."

"Why won't you just go away?"

No way would he answer that question truthfully. This was a familiar dodge on her part and he suspected she mostly said it by rote. Besides, she probably wasn't quite ready to hear that he was falling in love with her, that he hoped she'd love him back. And it had nothing to do with the fact she was having his babies. He'd been mooning over her long before he discovered her bombshell. "Because I'm here to stay."

"Gah. Don't make rhymes." She paused to twirl spaghetti around her fork, then ate it. "What about your other baby mama?"

"She's not my baby mama. I'll remind you that the prenatal DNA test cleared me completely. As soon as Chance threatened to countersue, she agreed to the test and then dropped her suit."

She shook her hand loose and concentrated on eating. He let a few minutes of silence pass before speaking again. "Spend the holidays with me."

"I can't." Did she sound disappointed?

"Why not?"

"I told you before, I have plans."

"Change them."

"I can't."

"Can't or won't?"

"Both." She set down her fork and now she studied him.

"Why not?"

"We're too different."

"How so?"

"You're…old-fashioned."

"That's a bad thing?"

"You drive me crazy."

"You'll never be bored and since you're something of an adrenaline junky…" He deliberately let his voice trail off. That was a very touchy subject for them both.

"Face it, Coop. Things will never work between us. You have to know that."

"I know nothing of the sort."

Twelve

I know nothing of the sort.

Cooper's assertion had been ricocheting around in Britt's head for two weeks now—two weeks that she'd managed to avoid his calls and texts. She'd steered clear of his big family Christmas. She used the time to herself to work on her dissertation and avoid temptation. With classes at the university on winter break and storm chasing on hold because of the mild weather, she'd finished the first draft. She missed the thrill of the chase and so long as she had no complications, her doctor said she could continue.

She'd also learned that the documentary she and Leo had put together was up for a regional Emmy. With the awards gala a week away, she'd broken down and gone shopping. Her blue formal from November no longer fit and while she didn't believe she had a snowball's chance in hell to win, she wanted to look…pretty.

Not that anyone would notice. Sure, Leo and she were going together. So was his wife. She didn't have a plus-one on standby. Other than Cooper. And no way was she going to involve him any deeper in her life. Coming to depend on him wasn't a good idea. She was an independent woman and she would do this on her own terms.

Britt rubbed at her temple with the fingers of her left hand while she stroked the side of her belly with her right. The twins were more active and it seemed her stomach had ballooned almost overnight. She hadn't felt pretty at all in any of the dresses she tried on. So now she was taking a break at Cadie B's Southern Kitchen in Bricktown. She sat at a table near the windows overlooking the canal patio.

"Mind if I join you?"

Startled, Britt jerked her head around. Katherine Tate was already pulling out the chair across from her and settling into it. "Um…" She blinked several times, gathering her thoughts. "I guess not since you're already sitting, Mrs. Tate."

The older woman's frosty smile would have unnerved Britt but for the momentary twinkle in Mrs. Tate's eyes.

A waitress approached with a menu but Mrs. Tate waved it away. "You've already ordered?" Britt nodded mutely. Mrs. Tate smiled at the waitress. "I want today's special, water with lemon, and coffee."

Silence stretched between them until the water and

coffee had been served. Britt, her nerves stretched tight, opened her mouth but snapped it shut when Katherine spoke.

"Please call me Katherine. You are, after all, carrying my grandbabies."

Shocked speechless, Britt stared at Cooper's mother. Her head tilted, almost of its own accord, and her lips pursed. All sorts of thoughts raced between her brain and her mouth while she attempted to form a complete sentence that would sound coherent.

"Something you will learn about me, Britt. I don't play around. I speak my mind and I appreciate others who do the same."

"Okay." Britt stretched out the word, scrambling for something even semi-intelligent to say. If Mrs. Tate could be blunt, so could she. "You've surprised me. I'd think that you would at least question my veracity and motives."

"I know my son moped around for months and suddenly, he sees you at the fund-raiser and perks right up. I also know that his brothers and cousins remain... skeptical."

"But you aren't?"

"No. When that man accused Cooper and his sister filed that lawsuit, my son vehemently denied even knowing the woman. You?" Katherine inclined her head slightly in Britt's direction. "You he pursues with a single-minded intensity that reminds me of his father. It's like that with the Tate men. When they fall, they fall hard. And they fall only once."

Britt eyed the older woman, bewildered by Mrs.

Tate's demeanor and the entire gist of this conversation. Her brain scrambled for an excuse she could use to extricate herself. No subterfuge came to mind so she chose bluntness.

"Why are you telling me this?"

Katherine fingered the pearls around her neck but didn't speak. Britt attempted to wait out the other woman, but impatience got the best of her. "Look, I don't like to play games either. I don't want your son. And I don't need him."

"Would you have told him if he hadn't discovered your condition on his own?"

"On his own? I told him." Even if she hadn't wanted to.

"After he found out you were pregnant and put two and two together."

"Fine. I had my doubts, especially after that scene at the museum during the gala. I figured if I told him, he'd want nothing to do with me. And that works just fine and dandy for me because..." She leaned forward, her gaze holding the other woman's while she very carefully enunciated each word. "I don't want anything from him."

"You don't?"

"No."

"Are you sure?"

She gaped. "Am I sure? Of course I'm sure. The only reason I waited to tell Cooper in the first place—"

"Is because he pinned you down."

"No, I would have told him." She blew out a breath and barely resisted rolling her eyes. "Fine. Still, I would have told him eventually because he had a right to know. You can tell your bullheaded son that getting married just because I'm pregnant is a stupid idea." She held up a finger to stall the retort hovering on Katherine's lips because she had a full head of steam up. "Tell Hero Boy that I don't need or want him. The babies are half his so he can damn well pay his share of support but me? I'm off-limits."

Katherine's smile was smug. "You'll do, my girl. You'll do quite well indeed."

Britt leaned back in her chair, thankful the waitress appeared with their food. She'd do? What did that even mean? She took a bite, keeping a narrow-eyed gaze on Katherine. What was it about this family that they totally ignored anything they didn't want to hear.

Like mother, like son.

Cooper sat on the couch in Cash's office, his cousin's huge Newfoundland dog sprawled across his lap. He loved the big goof despite the drool and shedding hair but Lucifer would demand his pound of flesh—literally—for Coop's species betrayal. His mother and brother sat in two armchairs while Cash propped a hip against the back of the couch. They were there to discuss his latest intel on the Carringtons.

"We have more information about Alex and Colby," Cash began.

"Tell me what you've found out about Trey," Katherine said.

"Trey?" Cooper repeated.

"Colby. That was our nickname for him in college. I haven't seen him since then."

Cooper and Bridger both leaned toward their mother. "Mom? You knew him in college? You wanna explain?"

"No, Bridger, I do not."

"Aunt Kath—"

"No, Cash. I will not regale you boys with tales of my misspent youth. I will tell you this much. Trey was a young man far more interested in me than I was in him. I was at Radcliffe at the time. He was a Harvard student." She looked at Cash. "Your father stepped in when Trey wouldn't take the hint that I was not interested. Cyrus and I may not have seen eye-to-eye on much, but I did appreciate his intervention." She smiled fondly at her boys. "He especially didn't appreciate that I appeared to jump out of the frying pan and into the fire when I met your father. Denver—" Her eyes grew misty and her smile was both sad and fond. "Your father was my world."

The relationship between his mom's brother and patriarch of the Barron family, Cyrus Barron, and his dad had never been what anyone would call cordial. Cooper glanced up at his cousin. "So why do you think Alex was at the gala, and why did he approach Mom?"

"I don't know. He's still in town, though. Nosing around several of the Barron companies." Cash studied Katherine. "Colby Carrington is the CEO of CCI, Ltd. As near as Chase and I can figure out, it's a family-held conglomerate. His net worth is in the high seven figures. He inherited his money and the company. Alex is his middle son, with an MBA from Harvard Business School and a reputation as a corporate raider."

Cooper exchanged a long look with his brother before they both looked at their mother. Coop expressed what they were both thinking. "It could be a coincidence, but I don't like that he's poking around in our business."

"Neither do I." Cash was always blunt. "I plan to do a deeper dig on the whole family and their company." He studied the others before continuing. "CCI is headquartered in Hartford, Connecticut. I don't buy the fact that either Carrington is interested in investing here." His expression turned grim. "Aunt Katherine, what exactly did my father do to the senior Carrington?"

She sighed, her hand going to the strand of pearls around her neck, a gesture so familiar to Cooper that it was almost as comforting to him as it obviously was to her.

"Mom? We aren't dredging up the past for grins and giggles. There had to be a reason for his son to approach you the way he did. You said yourself that he introduced himself like you should know his name and pedigree. You obviously did, and I think it's smart you played reticent, but we need to figure out what's going on."

"I left Radcliffe after two years. Partly because I met your father and partly because the situation with Trey had become untenable. When I didn't return to school, Trey came out here looking for me. Cyrus had a rather stern talk with him and sent him back to Boston. It didn't last. He continued to write and to call me. And that spring break, he came back. Cyrus caught him. I don't know precisely what happened but—" She glanced up at Cash. "Your father's hands were bruised and battered. I suspect he gave Trey a serious beating, along with the threat that if he ever contacted me again, the authorities would never find his body."

Cooper was both shocked and impressed that his uncle had that in him. The guy had been ruthless as all get-out and didn't care who he cut off at the knees—including his own sons—but as far as Cooper knew, he'd never gotten his hands dirty like that.

"Wonder if the old guy has a screw loose?" Bridge added.

"Something to consider," Cash agreed. "You have your assignment, Bridge. Work with Chase and Tucker. He has contacts he can tap into. And get our IT folks on this."

"Roger that, boss."

"In other news…" Cash turned his attention to Cooper.

"In other news," Katherine interjected. "What are you doing about Britt Owens?"

Cooper stared at his mom. "Excuse me?"

"Britt and your babies. What are you doing about them?"

"I asked her to marry me." He ignored the shocked intakes of breath coming from his brother and cousin.

"She's not very happy with you."

Cooper had a very bad feeling about that statement. He eyed his mother warily. "How would you know?"

"I bought her lunch today. Did you know she likes to eat at Cadie B's?"

Snapping his mouth shut once he realized it was

hanging open, Cooper couldn't find words. Instead, he rubbed his forehead and squinted against the headache that was building. "Mom…" His tone was a warning.

"I just happened to be there and saw her eating alone. I wanted to get to know my future daughter-in-law. Independent little thing, isn't she."

That wasn't a question and he wasn't about to answer. He had the right to remain silent and with Katherine Tate for a mother, silence was always the best option.

She arched a brow at him. "I'm aware that she said no. You need to woo her, Cooper."

"Woo her?" Bridger stage-whispered before snickering. He sobered immediately when his mother turned to stare at him.

"It is unfortunate that she witnessed that little scene at the museum. You have your work cut out for you. Why didn't you invite her for Christmas?"

Cooper unconsciously rubbed his jaw where he'd been coldcocked at the gala then dropped his hand when he realized he was doing so. "I did."

"Why didn't she accept?"

"Why do you think?"

"She had other plans, even if those were sitting alone in her apartment." His mother pushed out of the chair and headed toward the door, apparently done with them all. She paused and looked back. "Fix this, Cooper."

Thirteen

Chase stared at him. "You can't be serious, Coop. This is kind of a big deal—at least to those who are up for the awards. I can get you in. That's easy, even with short notice, since the event is being held at the Crown Barron."

Well aware that the ceremony to present regional Emmys was being held in Oklahoma City at the family-owned hotel, Coop shrugged. "That'd be no fun."

"And crashing her party will be?"

His cousin had a point and he would need assistance to be seated at Channel 2's table, but he wanted Britt to be surprised and off balance—especially since she hadn't mentioned she'd been nominated and had been doing her best to avoid him. She and Leo had put together a thirty-minute documentary on storm chasers that showed how what they did as reporters was far more than just going after tornadoes. In fact, Cooper was featured in some of the footage from that November wildfire. He'd been down in the Gulf dealing with a new rig when it had aired. His mother DVR'd it for him to watch.

Britt's voice-overs and her eye for picking the most dramatic footage were amazing. He just didn't understand why she fought going in front of the camera as an in-studio personality. He wasn't an adrenaline junkie, but he got the appeal of her work. Except she was pregnant. The argument over storm chasing in her condition was ongoing.

"Just get me in, Chase. Without Britt finding out I'm going to be there."

"Black tie, dude. Just sayin'. I know how much you *love* dressing up."

For Britt? He'd wear anything. Heck, he'd walk around the bases at the Bricktown Ballpark buck naked in front of a sellout crowd if she asked. "My tux is cleaned and pressed."

"Whatever."

Savannah, Chase's wife, made a *tsking* sound. "You realize that we have to vet her, don't you? Make sure she's good enough for you?" She flashed both men a cheeky grin. "And personally? I think you surprising her is awesome. Ooh..." Her twinkling eyes landed on her husband. "If we knew for sure that she's the winner, you could arrange to have Cooper present it to her. How awesome would that be?"

Cooper choked and turned a wide-eyed stare on her. "Don't. Just...no, Savvie. If the Bee Dubyas get anywhere near her, I swear to heaven I will come hunting all of you and you won't like the consequences. I'm having enough trouble wrangling her without y'all's interference."

"We don't interfere—"

"The hell you don't," Chase muttered under his breath. Louder, he added, "Darlin', just stay out of this one. It's way more complicated than y'all think."

"Well, duh, Chase." Savvie rolled her eyes this time. "We *are* aware that she's carrying his twins. What we want to know is why she thinks she's too good for him."

Groaning, Cooper dropped his head into the palm of his hand. "Please, Savannah. If you love Chase, stay out of my life. And keep your sisters-in-law away too."

"Hey, we help!"

"No!" Cooper and Chase exclaimed at the same time.

She huffed and crinkled her nose. "Fine. You'll be sorry, and when you come crawling back asking us to get involved to save your sorry tail, we'll just laugh at you."

Unsure whether he should be relieved or apprehensive, Cooper dipped his chin in acknowledgment. "Thank you."

His phone pinged and after reading the message, he headed toward the door of Chase's office. "Thanks, cuz."

"Don't thank me, Coop. *I* think this is a dumb idea and the fact that my wife thinks it's a good one? Yeah, I'd be running fast and far if I were you, bud."

Britt stepped out of the limo provided by KOCX with help from Leo. Her truck was so much easier to get in and out of, even with the extra frontal protrusion. She patted her belly to remind the babies that she loved them despite her often snarky thoughts concerning them. Looking up, she realized there was a red carpet. A *real* red carpet with red velvet ropes keeping the photographers and fans away. Granted, it was nothing like Hollywood, but a little zing ran up her spine. She was glad the temperatures had turned mild for January so she didn't need a coat.

The doors to the historic Barron Crown Hotel swung wide. She, Leo and his wife walked through them. People milled about the lobby, following the trail of the red carpet. Deeper inside, a backdrop had been erected and everyone paused to have their photographs taken. She stood there a little dumbfounded and slightly starstruck. Someone touched the small of her back and urged her forward.

"This way, Ms. Owens."

Heat licked at her skin. She knew that touch *and* the voice. Cooper! What was he doing here? She marched forward, quickening her step to draw away from the weight of his hand.

"Easy, Girl Wonder. You're wearing heels. Wouldn't want you to get tripped up."

His voice, like smooth caramel, poured over her. She'd managed to avoid him—mostly—for almost a month. It hadn't been easy. But she should have realized he'd try to pull a stunt like this. He just wasn't giving up. She almost had to give the guy props for his stubbornness, and deep down, it made her feel all mushy.

Cooper's arm slid around her waist, pulling her up

short, dead center of the backdrop. He leaned over to whisper into her ear. “Smile for the camera, darlin’.”

“Don’t *darlin’* me,” she snarled, right as the flash went off, blinding her for a moment. She closed her eyes to clear the sparkles.

“You are sooo gonna pay for this,” she hissed under her breath. So much for those mushy feelings.

“I can think of all sorts of ways I can do that,” he teased. Her skin flushed, the chemistry between them flaring white-hot. Her memory was far too good, and now that he’d put the thought in her head, her imagination was far too vivid.

She clamped her mouth shut, refusing to give him any more ammunition. Ever since he’d confirmed that she was pregnant, he’d been tracking her like a bloodhound. No. Bloodhounds were cute and cuddly. Cooper Tate was a wolf, pure and simple. A big, bad wolf. Who would use his big teeth and big paws and big everything else on her. She shivered and Cooper put his arm around her shoulders. Like it was the most natural thing in the world, she leaned into his warmth as he led her toward the ballroom where the gala was happening.

“Cold?”

“No.”

She caught his knowing smile from the corner of her eye and let out a silent *argh.* Why had she ever told him that she was pregnant? And why couldn’t he just be a jerk, offer her child support and stay far away? No, he had to be all gentlemanly and insist on marrying her. He didn’t love her, and they mixed together like baking soda and vinegar with explosive results. They’d be divorced within a year and then where would the babies be?

Babies. Twins. Britt was still getting used to that idea. They didn't run in her family so it was all Cooper's fault. And she'd told him that on numerous occasions. The big jerk just puffed out his chest and claimed it was that potent Barron and Tate blood running in his veins.

Still, he was so dang handsome as he stood there beside her in his formal attire. His white tux coat was longer than other men's, with short lapels, three buttons, and a squared-off lower hem that hit him about midthigh on his black pants. She figured there was some fancy name for the style but she had no clue what it was. She did know that the style fit his broad shoulders and chest, and narrower waist and hips, to perfection. His vest was a slate gray and his tie was metallic silver. The black Stetson with the silver hatband sat atop his head like it had been created just for him. For all she knew, it had. Oil tycoon, she reminded herself. The whole outfit had probably been tailor-made.

They entered the ballroom and she stopped for a moment. The room looked like a set straight out of the glamorous early days of Hollywood—all white and silver art deco decorations and satin tablecloths and chair covers with big bows. Silver stars glittered behind billowing silk suspended along the arched ceiling, lit by gorgeous crystal chandeliers. Each round table held place settings of heavy silver flatware with snowy napkins folded into fantastical shapes with shiny silver chargers. Long stems of creamy calla lilies graced tall clear crystal vases, held by silver stones in the bottom.

And it struck her that Cooper fit in perfectly while she felt like a whale out of water.

"Wow," she breathed.

Wow indeed, Coop thought. When she'd first stepped out of the limo, his chest ached at the sight of her. First he caught sight of a strappy, high-heeled silver shoe, then a skirt made from something sheer and billowy in a color that rivaled expensive champagne. The long-sleeved top of the dress was covered in silver sequins, and a man's eyes traveled to the lovely woman wearing it, not her obvious rounded belly. He knew very little about women's fashions but Britt looked like a dream. She'd pulled her hair back, leaving a few strands loose to curl around her face.

He'd had to grit his teeth as Leo helped her out. Leo was a good guy and Coop had recruited the other man to help out in his pursuit of Britt. He'd waited just inside the door and claimed her as soon as she entered.

Now they were in the ballroom and stars gleamed in her blue eyes. She'd tucked her glasses into the small purse she carried and, after looking around surreptitiously, she fished them out. Settling them on her face, she surveyed the area a second time. Her lips formed a perfect O as she inhaled deeply and let out her breath before surreptitiously stuffing her glasses back in her purse.

"Pretty swanky, huh?"

"Amazing."

A waiter with a tray of champagne flutes approached. Coop grabbed a glass with one hand while leaning close to whisper in the waiter's ear and slipping a folded bill into the man's pocket. The waiter promptly disappeared but returned moments later with a refilled tray and one flute in his hand.

"For the lady," he said holding out the flute. It contained a liquid that was a slightly different color than the champagne in the rest of the glasses.

"Ginger ale," Coop explained. Britt happily accepted the drink. He nodded toward a table near the small stage set at the far end of the room. "Do you need to sit or would you like to wander around and schmooze."

She laughed softly. "That's a word I never thought to hear coming from your mouth."

He shrugged. "I have rich cousins and a socially conscious mother. I get dragged to a lot of events. I also work for one of the biggest family-held energy companies in the US. Schmoozing was a required class in my family education."

Britt curled her lips to keep from laughing again. Cooper wanted to kiss her. Well, he really wanted to do all sorts of things to her. She looked different without her glasses and with her hair so prim and styled. He wanted to pull the pins out of the bun and bury his fingers in her blond curls while he kissed her until neither of them could breathe. Britt always turned him on, usually at the most inopportune times. Like now. With people milling about and a lot of his family present. The public would frown on him going all caveman by scooping her up into his arms and making off with her. But the Barrons had a suite in the hotel and he had the security code to get into it. One elevator ride and they'd be on their way to a really good night.

He gazed down at her, the brim of his hat putting both of their faces into deeper shadows. Cooper wanted more than just a few nights with her. He'd known it all along. This was the woman for him. Now and always. All he had to do was convince her.

"Big night for you."

Britt inhaled deeply. "We won't win. I've been working on my happy face so I can congratulate the winner."

"I've got faith in you."

She blinked up at him, her expression softening. "Really?"

"Truly." He brushed his fingertips across her cheek and smiled when she leaned into the caress. In a very soft voice, he asked, "When are you going to marry me, Girl Wonder?"

Fourteen

Britt forced air into her constricted lungs. She hadn't expected him to bring up the subject again, especially not in this setting. Between the man and her hormones, her emotions were all over the map. When things were good between them, they were very, very good. Too good. Her fingers curled with the urge to touch him and the lips she bit tingled at the thought of kissing him. He was handsome enough to be a Hollywood star. And rich. With a perfect house and a perfect life. Just like their sexual chemistry was too good, he was too perfect. And she wasn't.

"Never. And you need to get over your hero complex. I don't need rescuing."

His expression hardened just enough that she noticed the tightening around his eyes and the slight downturn of his mouth. This was not a man to cross. He might appear easygoing but she'd caught the fierce determination he harbored on more than one occasion.

Before things got more uncomfortable, a man who looked very much like Cooper walked up with a dark-haired woman. Their identities clicked in her memory: Tucker Tate and his wife, country singer Zoe Parker. Zoe, evidently, was one to get directly to the point.

"When ya due, sweetie? And if it's not in a month or two, I hope there's not more than two buns in your oven."

She'd hoped that this dress, designed for a maternity collection and with its empire waist and flowing tulle skirt, would have partially disguised her condition. Obviously not. She pasted a fake smile on her face. Technically, Tucker was her great-granddaddy boss or something. He was the chief operations officer of Barron Entertainment, which owned KOCX. Even so, she couldn't keep a hint of sarcasm out of her voice when she responded. "How *sweet* of you to notice, *hon*. The twins are due in early June."

As if they didn't already know this. She doubted her involvement with Cooper was any great secret in the Tate family. Or among the Barrons, for that matter. She had the distinct impression that there were no secrets in that family.

Britt was surprised when Zoe didn't take offense at her sarcasm. "If those babies are anything like my Nash, you have all my sympathy, sugar." The woman glanced up at Tucker, eyes dancing with mischief. "And I just wanted to tell you that I've seen your documentary.

We don't get quite so much wild weather in Tennessee so I surely do admire the work you do, Britt. Crossin' m'fingers that you win tonight." She slipped her hand through her husband's arm.

Something inside Britt twisted just a little at the look on Tucker's face as he gazed down at his wife, his expression both amused and indulgent. "What Zoe is too reticent—"

"Honey, there's not a reticent bone in my body, and you know it. What I'm leadin' up to is I would dearly love to ride along with you when you go storm chasin'. I know Mama Katherine, using Coop's name, won your silent auction prize at the benefit last November. I asked him to let me do it and he flat out said no. So..." Zoe batted long lashes at Britt, who had to suppress a laugh.

Zoe was not at all what she'd expected. She truly was a country sweetheart and while Britt suspected the other woman could hold a mean grudge, there appeared to be nothing two-faced about her. This was someone—despite Zoe's fame and fortune—whom Britt could be friends with. She pretended to consider the idea, one arm resting on her belly, hand cupping the opposite elbow, while tapping her cheek with one finger in the classic I'm-thinking-about-it gesture.

Britt had all but forgotten about that stupid silent auction. Cooper hadn't pressed things and she now wondered if he was keeping it as a backup plan or something. That would be just like him, to use the ride-along to get close to her. Still, taking a singing star on a chase would bring lots of publicity and she had a secret fangirl crush on Zoe. She'd downloaded the singer's album the first day it was available. And what a way to derail any nefarious plans Cooper might have regarding their ride-along.

"Well...if you promise to sing to me, *and* give me an autograph, I bet we can work something out."

Zoe squealed and bounced up and down on her toes like a bobber on a cane fishing pole. That's when Britt realized the woman wore cowboy boots with her obviously expensive designer gown. Zoe looked like the girl next door with her long brown hair and big brown eyes. The dress? It was pure red carpet—flounced in front, long in back, some décolletage showing beneath the coppery sheer fabric. Pair that with fabulous boots as shiny as brand-new copper pennies, and she looked like she was ready to accept an award at the CMAs. The thought hit her that if she married Cooper, Zoe would be her sister-in-law. And Deacon Tate, the country music megastar, would be her brother-in-law. She started to hyperventilate. These people were so out of her league.

She had student loans out the wazoo, for Pete's sake. And just who was Pete, she wondered, the distraction helping to bring her breathing back under control. She licked her lips nervously as the three people surrounding her watched, worry evident in their expressions.

"Don't mind me." She waved one hand. "Nerves. I'm just a little anxious about the awards tonight." A good enough alibi, she hoped.

The overhead lights flashed, like in a theater lobby, to remind the patrons to return to their seats after intermission. Tucker and Zoe led the way. Britt followed with Cooper beside her, his warm hand resting against the small of her back. Heat spread through her and she fought against the magnetic pull of him—physically *and* emotionally. Cooper's breathing hitched, almost as if he felt the small tremors his touch evoked in her. Did he feel the same things she did? Was it possible that she was fighting her feelings for no reason?

As he held a chair for her and she sank onto it, she pushed those thoughts away. Deep down, she knew Cooper had the power to destroy her. He could take her job and attempt to take her babies. She could find another job but her children? She'd fight tooth and nail for them. But as she stroked her hand over her rounded belly, she knew Cooper would never do that to her. She glanced up and saw yearning in his gaze as he watched her touch her tummy.

He leaned in and whispered in her ear. "Everything okay? They giving you trouble tonight?"

"Not really." She studied him for a moment, made up her mind. "Want to touch?"

He dropped into the chair beside her and she guided his hand to her side. One of the babies chose that moment to kick hard. Cooper's eyes widened and a look of such wonder crossed his face that Zoe completely second-guessed her decisions. He was the father of the twins. He'd stepped up as soon as he became aware of that fact. And watching his reaction now? She knew deep in her heart that he truly wanted the babies. And maybe, he wanted her too.

Cooper remembered to breathe. He'd seen the twins moving on the sonograms but he'd never actually touched Britt's belly after he was aware of them being inside her. He'd felt that kick through her hand. Strong, powerful. And alive. It really hit him in that moment. Oh, he'd had a bit of a revelation when he'd seen them on that big screen at the doctor's office, but this? This contact, knowing his babies were in there growing and thriving, was amazing. Two little people that were half Britt and half him. He hoped they got her brains. Her stubbornness? Not so much. And if they were girls, he wanted them to look just like their mother. He was also guy enough to hope that they took after him if they were boys. Except he still wanted them to have Britt's intelligence.

"Wow," he finally said, moving his gaze from their hands to her face. Then he blinked and almost choked. "Does that hurt?" He'd never considered that it might and he never wanted to see Britt in pain.

She rolled her eyes at him but for the first time in ages, her expression was soft as she regarded him. "No, it doesn't hurt. Not exactly. It feels sort of like this." She punched him in the ribs, none too gently.

He grinned at her, but the wonder remained. He was going to be a dad. Before he could say anything else, the room darkened and the emcee began the ceremony. Cooper remained lost in a fog of happiness until he felt Britt stiffen beside him. He tuned back into his surroundings and noticed that everyone at their table sat up straight, anticipatory tension in their postures, as Britt's category was announced.

"*Chasing Down the Wind*, KOCX TV, Britt Owens and Leo Blevins."

The presenters went on to the other nominees but Cooper wasn't paying any attention. Not when Britt's hand had a death grip on his thigh. He carefully loosened her hold, substituting his hand. At long last, the woman at the microphone said, "And the winner is…"

The male emcee tore open the envelope he held, pulled out the embossed card, and smiling, leaned toward the microphone and announced, "Chasing Down the Wind." He went on to read all the names involved.

Britt squealed as Leo let out a whoop. He kissed his wife and before Cooper knew it, Britt was kissing him. After a long moment, she pulled away, looking surprised with herself.

"Congratulations, Girl Wonder. Proud of you." And he wasn't lying. He *was* proud of her. He just didn't want her putting herself in danger.

He pushed out of his chair and helped her stand. Everyone at the table stood with him, all of them clapping and whistling as Britt and Leo headed to the small platform, followed by a producer and Dave Edmonds, the station's head meteorologist.

Everyone gave a quick acceptance speech, passing the golden Emmy statuette around as each one spoke. Then the group was ushered off to the side where they posed for photographs as the next award was announced. Within a few minutes, they'd returned to the table for another round of congratulations. The rest of the ceremony went by in a blur.

Once things wrapped up, Cooper put his plan into action—mainly getting rid of his brother and sister-in-law, sending Leo and his wife home in the limo, and bustling Britt into his brand-new Lincoln Navigator. The only delay was a game of rock-paper-scissors between Britt and Leo to determine who got to take the Emmy home for the night. Lucky—or intelligently conniving—as always, Britt won.

Inside the Navigator, with the heat blasting, he glanced at her, and was surprised to find her studying him. "Penny for your thoughts..."

"It's a dollar now. Inflation and all that." She smiled when he pulled out a dollar bill. "Funny."

"Britt..."

"Cooper..."

His turn to smile now. "Will you come home with me?" He glanced away from her to focus on driving. "We'll put that shiny statuette on the mantel, build a fire in the fireplace, snuggle in on the couch and admire it."

"Sure we will." Britt touched his arm and he looked at her. She winked at him and he breathed. "Yes, I'll go home with you."

When Britt opened her eyes, gray winter sunlight drifted through the filmy drapes curtaining the French doors and casting a golden glow on the statuette prominently displayed on Cooper's bedside table. She'd won a freaking Emmy! And...she'd slept with Cooper. Again. Despite her best intentions, she couldn't stay away from him.

Her dilemma currently snored softly at her back, one arm draped over her and a warm hand cupping her belly.

She shivered when lips nuzzled the nape of her neck. "You like my house," Cooper murmured against her skin.

"Maybe a little." She could admit that much but wasn't about to tell him she thought his house was perfect.

"I like having you here." His hand caressed her side. "You could live here…"

"I don't think so."

"Why not?"

"You know all the reasons, Cooper."

Their cell phones both beeped alerts. Since his arms were around her, Britt reached for hers. The banner text made her sit up, swing her legs out of bed and head for the windows. A winter not-so-wonderland stretched out before her.

"What the—" There hadn't been an ice storm in the forecast. A cold front had been predicted for the start of the week but not overnight. This was why weather fascinated her.

Cooper joined her at the window. He offered her a long-sleeved T-shirt, even though the air in the room was warm. He helped her into it and she smiled at the sweet gesture. The shirt swallowed her, the sleeves trailing way over her hands and the bottom hem falling to midthigh. When he kissed her temple, she didn't shy away.

"I'm going to grab a quick shower then I'll start coffee and breakfast. Take your time. I've got some calls to make."

She tilted her head to look up at him. "It's Sunday morning."

"And we woke up to an ice storm. Half the state is shut down and I have active rigs in the alert area. I need to make sure my crews are okay."

Britt had never considered exactly what Cooper did. In the back of her mind, he was just some rich oil executive with a corner office in Barron Tower. Except he traveled to hurricane zones and volunteered with the Cajun Navy. He drove bulldozers and rescued trapped cows—cattle, she amended. He *did* things. Physical things that got his hands dirty. Literally. He rescued her and he lived in a perfect house on a perfect acreage and he cradled her while she slept.

And her resistance was beginning to crumble.

Fifteen

After two months, Cooper should have been used to this. He was waiting in the kitchen when she walked in just past five o'clock. "You snuck out again this morning." He kept his voice level, not that he was really upset. Okay, maybe just a little. She made a habit of sneaking out and he always woke up disgruntled when he found her side of the bed empty. After the three-day ice storm back in January, most of her clothes had slowly migrated from her apartment to his closet, along with some personal items over that time. She was all but living with him but she would not, despite all his best efforts, admit that she was.

"I had to be at work at eight." She bristled, arms folded across the large swell of her belly.

He raised a brow. Britt raised her chin. He had to

be a truly sick puppy to enjoy her stubborn temper as much as he did. "So?"

She gave him the stink eye, arms crossed, feet splayed for balance as she leaned toward him.

"I didn't want to be late."

"How long would it take to wake me with a kiss and tell me goodbye?"

Color rose up her neck to eventually stain her cheeks. He liked that he had that effect on her.

"You don't do '*goodbye*' kisses." Her hands came up to make air quotes.

"I don't?"

She waggled a finger. "No, you don't. You start with a kiss and then you get all grabby hands and…and… I'm suddenly naked and late. I'm not a big boss like you. I'm a lowly adjunct professor, and part-time at that. I can't afford to be late and it's a longer drive from your house."

Britt was gearing up for a tirade and whatever happened next was sure to be entertaining. He added fuel to the fire. "I'm sure the powers that be at the station would hire you full time for in-studio stuff. That pays more than being an adjunct professor and you wouldn't have to drive all the way to Norman."

"I *like* teaching. And I'm not the anchor type."

"Working at the TV station means no rush hour traffic."

"I hate it when you're logical," she groused.

"Then I'll be illogical. Marry me and quit."

"Don't even go there. Just because I'm pregnant—"

"I love you."

Her eyes softened and he had hope until she spoke.

"I don't love you, Cooper."

"You will."

"Don't be so sure."

He used his boyish grin, the one that hinted at a dimple he didn't really have but always drove the girls crazy. "I'll wear you down eventually."

That got him an exaggerated eye roll. Part of him knew better than to push her but he was getting tired of the long game. As much as Britt frustrated him, he also adored her. Of course he was in love with her. How could he not be?

"Are you hungry?"

Britt looked confused for a minute. "What?"

"Dinner. I can cook or we can go out."

"I think I just got whiplash from the change in subject. And I can cook."

"You look tired. Why don't you put your feet up and I'll fix something."

"You're changing the subject because you were losing the argument."

"I was winning but you do look tired."

"You're coddling me again, thinking it'll help your cause."

"Yes, yes I am. Is it working?"

"No." She huffed out a breath. "Maybe."

He'd take that.

Britt settled on a bale of hay in Cooper's horse barn. March had roared in like a lion but was currently playing the lamb. Bored, she'd trailed after Cooper when he headed outside with a casual, "Got chores to do," called over his shoulder.

She wasn't much of a country girl but hey, hay was hay, right? Horse and cow food and a place to sit while she watched Cooper brush a big gray horse. Yes, that summed up hay nicely. And was about as deep as her thoughts could get at the moment. Cooper wore a heather-gray T-shirt that molded to his body. Faded jeans hugged his butt and every time he bent over, she had to swallow the saliva pooling in her mouth. Why was he so sexy? And such a nice guy. She really needed him to be a big ol' jerk because her heart was at stake, which it shouldn't be. They shouldn't hook up just because they were going to be parents.

Granted, they'd had a series of one-night stands, which stretched into a series of one-week stands and now it was almost April. She had no excuse for her actions. They had nothing in common. He was rich. *Really* rich. He belonged to a powerful family. He looked as good in old jeans and a T-shirt as he did in a designer suit and that, she decided, was a tough act to follow. He tripped her feminine switches with his rugged, outdoorsy good looks. He always had. She'd all but thrown herself at him—okay, she *had* thrown herself at him like five minutes after she first saw him.

He should be a jerk, she reminded herself. But he wasn't. She watched the muscles of his arm bunch and relax as he brushed the horse, concentrating on that rather than his broad back. Little shivers teased through her body. Why had he turned out to be a really good guy? The good ones were supposed to be as rare as unicorns.

"What's her name?" Britt had to focus on something besides the man.

"His. This is Tramp. He's a gelding."

"Okay…"

Cooper glanced over at her. "Three kinds of horses, Girl Wonder." He held up an index finger. "Mares. Those are the female horses."

"I knew that," she muttered.

"Stallions," he said, holding up a second finger.

"Know that, too."

"And geldings. Who used to be stallions."

"That's weird. When dogs are neutered, they're still just dogs."

"It's the same with cattle. A bull that's been cut is a steer."

"Cut?"

"That's the cowboy term for neutering a horse or cow."

"I thought a cow was female. So you spay cows?"

"Cow is the singular term for any bovine. It is also a female cow, as opposed to a bull or steer."

"Stop. You're going to make my head explode."

He moved around the horse to brush the other side, watching her over the big animal's back. "Okay. I won't explain about calves and heifers or colts and fillies then."

She glowered and moved her curled hands up to both sides of her head and expanded them with sound effects to indicate that her head had, indeed, exploded, at least figuratively.

"And then there's—"

"Shut up, Coop. Just…shut it."

The grin he flashed was full of wicked intent. "Make me."

"I can do that," she said, her own expression just as wicked.

A few days later, Britt stood in the archway separating the dining room and kitchen. Cooper sat at the high counter dividing the kitchen from the family room spooning something into his mouth. Her eyes narrowed as she recognized the fragrance that had enticed her.

"Did you leave any for me?"

Cooper's head jerked up, his expression bathed in guilt. Britt managed a poker face though it was hard to resist curling her lips between her teeth to keep from smiling. The empty dish spoke volumes—as did the empty container proclaiming it had once held vanilla bean ice cream. He slid off the stool and padded over to the refrigerator. His faded jeans rode low on his hips, his back flaring into broad shoulders. *Nope.* She wouldn't be distracted by his obvious charms. She was not going there. Especially since he'd eaten her peach cobbler.

His head and shoulders disappeared into the fridge and he withdrew something. Then the freezer drawer opened, closed. He kept his back to her but said, "Have a seat, Girl Wonder. You need real food."

Britt *humphed* but settled on the stool he'd vacated. She glanced at the bowl he'd been eating from. A pool of melted ice cream and a smear of gooey sauce left from the cobbler was all that remained of the treat his mother had dropped by. For her. Not Cooper. For Britt. She knew that because Katherine had called her to say she was dropping off a peach cobbler just for her because it was her favorite. She absently rubbed the side of her rounded belly. One of the twins was using her rib cage for a jungle gym.

A chef's salad appeared in front of her. "Eat all of that and you get dessert."

Coop held another cobbler and carton of ice cream.

"Tease," she groused.

"Absolutely."

She poured blue cheese dressing over the salad, impressed that he'd cut the hard-boiled eggs into precise slices. Even the fresh ham and turkey had been julienned. And there wasn't a tomato in sight. She had nothing against tomatoes. They were perfectly nice as long as they involved ketchup, spaghetti sauce or BBQ. For a man who seemed mostly clueless, Cooper sure did pay attention when it came to her likes and dislikes. She stabbed at some leafy greens and swirled them through the dressing. She was chewing when Coop set down a napkin-covered basket. Hot breadsticks hid beneath the cloth. Who used cloth napkins? Well, what bachelor used them? Besides Cooper Tate, obviously.

Of course, she'd met—and been vetted—by Katherine Tate. The woman wore pearls, for gosh sakes. *Of course* there would be no paper napkins on her table. Britt preferred paper towels herself. Then again, she hadn't exactly eaten at home. She dined a la carte—

from Taco Bell, Sonic, KFC, Arby's. Fast food was definitely her cuisine of choice. Since all but moving in with Cooper, though, they often ate at home, usually with him cooking. Living here was easy to get used to. And she shouldn't. A part of her kept waiting for that proverbial other shoe—or in this case, boot—to drop.

A dark shadow appeared on the opposite wall and she watched as Lucifer slunk toward her. The cat was a sneaky devil and he loved ice cream. She wondered if he liked cobbler. She shoveled salad into her mouth. A strip of ham fell off her fork and didn't make it to the floor. Luci caught it midair and scarfed it down. Then he sat back on his haunches gazing at her with a baleful expression, demanding she drop more meat.

"Don't feed the cat. He has his own bowl."

She glanced up, her guilt apparently obvious on her face, based on Cooper's grin.

"Whatever," she muttered. But there was warm peach cobbler and ice cream to distract her from the sexy man.

Cooper had hung the swing from the big tree near the fire pit on a whim. With his cousins' children coming for the occasional visit, it seemed like a good idea at the time. Now? Now, he decided the idea had been utterly brilliant. Britt, wearing a loose dress covered with flowers painted in outrageous hues, pushed off in the swing. Her rounded belly peeked from behind the riotous colors as she pumped her legs and leaned back to swing higher.

For all intents and purposes, they were living together. He liked having her under his roof and in his life. A rough meow drew his attention to his feet. Lucifer sat beside his scuffed boots, eyes fixed on the colorful display. Britt continued to swing gently, her barefoot toes reaching for the sky on the upswing, in dappled shade for a moment before they disappeared in the long skirt as she folded them beneath the swing on her way back down.

He moved closer, standing by just in case. He would give her a push whenever she asked, whenever she hollered, "Higher!" She didn't ask so he remained on the sidelines with Lucifer. "We need to figure out a way to make her stay," he muttered to the cat. He glanced down. Luci stared up at him, his gaze malevolent. "You know you want her to stay just as much as I do."

In a display of feline disgust, Luci appeared to roll his eyes as he shook his head, flipped his tail and sauntered back toward the main house. The cat couldn't fool him. He'd caught the darn thing curled up next to Britt, snore-purring while she petted him, more than once.

Cooper settled into a lounge chair and watched the woman he hungered for. The sun disappeared as gray clouds collided overhead. The wind changed, bringing the scent of rain and ozone. Britt slowed the swing, dragging her feet in the grass until it stopped. She hopped out and strode toward him, calling "Where's my phone?"

He pulled it out of his hip pocket and handed it to her. As she checked for messages, the first fat raindrops fell. Coop grabbed her hand and pulled her toward the house. They were drenched by the time they reached the French door opening into the master bedroom. Laughing like kids, they surged into the house and headed to the bath. He grabbed a thick towel and wrapped it around her before snagging a second one he used to dry her long hair.

"What about you?" Britt asked, eyeing the way his shirt molded to his chest.

"I'm not so sweet that I'll melt because I got wet. You? You might."

Cooper didn't smile at first when he saw her expression go soft. But looking into brown eyes the color of melted chocolate, he felt his own expression soften.

"You shouldn't say things like that," Britt murmured.

"Why not?"

"Because you'll make me like you and I don't want to like you."

"You're carrying my babies, Britt. You should like me."

"No, I shouldn't," she insisted as she face-planted against his wet shirt. "You're a serial impregnator."

"I don't think that's a word."

"It should be."

He gently gripped her biceps and leaned away from her while keeping her in place. He met her gaze dead on. "I've never gotten anyone but you pregnant, Britt. And if I'd been thinking with the correct head, I would have realized the stupid condom was old."

"But that other woman is stuck in my head…"

"Shh." He released her arms, his hands moving to cup her face. He bent and brushed his lips across hers.

"I'll show you the DNA test if that will help. I promise, Britt. You are the only one carrying my children."

She rocked back and while he let her go, he didn't break eye contact. She studied him, her gaze flicking over his face, his body, then the area around them.

"You have a swing in your yard," she whispered.

"Yeah."

"I love swings." The soft expression on her face was replaced by one filled with worry. "Do you really want the twins?"

She sounded so fragile, not brash and sure like his Girl Wonder at all. "C'mere, sweetheart." He wrapped Britt in his arms, but he didn't answer her. Instead, he eased off her wet clothes and dried the damp left behind from the rain. Then he dressed her in one of his T-shirts and set her on the counter while he stripped and dried off before pulling on a pair a loose cotton gym shorts. Lifting her into his arms, he carried her to the bed.

They lay together, listening to the heavy patter of the rain, lightning occasionally flashing through the windows, followed by thunder. He stroked her lightly, and simply enjoyed holding her as they lay together.

Eventually, he spoke. "I have six cousins, all brothers by three different women. I have six brothers. Same mom and dad. Family is kind of a big deal around here. I was with Cord right after he learned about CJ. He was devastated that he'd missed so much of his son's life because Jolie didn't tell him. And Deacon? He didn't give a damn whether Noelle was his by blood or not. He became that little girl's dad the moment he picked her up. The same with Tucker. He didn't care that Zoe was having another guy's baby. He loves Zoe, and Nash is his. End of story. How could I not want our babies?"

"Your family is a little weird."

Laughter burst out before he could stop it, the explosion ruffling Britt's hair. "A little weird? Darlin', you don't know us at all. My mother wears pearls to ride horseback. My oldest brother is a super ninja dude, my baby brother is a musical genius, and the rest of us just hang on for the ride. Well, I just hold on for the ride because I'm the only normal and sane one in the bunch."

Britt giggled. "Deacon seems pretty squared away."

"Deacon is married to a former highway patrol trooper."

"So?"

"Who do you think keeps him squared away? I mean, dude. He's a Nashville country music superstar."

"You guys are all overachievers."

"I blame it on sibling rivalry."

"So what's your superpower?"

"Saving pretty storm chasers."

"I don't need saving."

Did her voice sound a little wistful? There beneath the indignation? Yeah, Cooper decided. He'd heard it. He settled her with her head on his shoulder so they could both watch the rain out the window. A comfortable silence stretched between them. After a while, the rain petered off. The delicate, sweet fragrance of honeysuckle washed in through the open windows on the fresh breeze. The storm rumbled in the distance as rain changed to drizzle. Though the storm had come to an end, neither of them moved. Daylight faded to dusk, but he didn't turn on a light.

"I love that scent," Britt finally said. "Rain and honeysuckle. It reminds me of spring."

He kissed the top of her head. "Rain and honeysuckle will always remind me of you."

"Stop saying stuff like that." She raised her head and twisted her neck to look at him. "Just stop being sweet."

"Ha," he teased. "You do like me."

Sixteen

There was always calm before the storm. They'd been getting along so well, but then again, they'd had a mild spring, Until now. Severe weather was out there waiting and Cooper realized he'd probably just stepped in a big ol' pile of cow patties when he decreed that she was not going to be chasing tornadoes this year.

"You have no right to tell me what I can and cannot do, Cooper Tate." Britt was spitting mad. "It's spring. Storm season. My job is to be out there—" She swept her arm in a wide arc indicating…the world. "This is what I do."

"You're pregnant."

She cupped her palms on both sides of her belly. "Gee. Brilliant deduction. What was your first clue, Sherlock?"

"Britt—"

"Do not go there, Cooper. Don't get all conciliatory and condescending. I'm perfectly healthy and thus capable of doing my job. My doctor has cleared me to work. The station has cleared me."

He inhaled to argue again but she cut him off. "I sit in my truck. I drive my truck. I look at instrument readings. I'd say I take pictures but that's what Leo is for. He'll be with me. He's perfectly capable of driving too. It's just that trying to work the cameras and the communications equipment is better done when not driving. I'm not due until June. This is April. Heck, the doctor said I could work right up to the point my water breaks."

Coop resisted the urge to stick his fingers in his ears and sing la-la-la-la like a six-year-old who didn't want to hear his parents. He'd undergone a crash course on pregnancy and childbirth with his cousin Kaden. Despite being squeamish, he was looking forward to the birth of his children. The little duo hadn't yet revealed their genders, and they were on the small side for how far along they were in the gestation period. He knew this because, yeah, he'd taken a *second* crash course because these were *his* babies. And he was ready for them. Sort of. Mostly. As ready as any man could be.

He swallowed his anger and tried logic instead. "You're having twins, Britt." He ignored the look she leveled on him. "The doctor said there is a chance you could go into premature labor. What happens if you are out in the middle of nowhere?"

"Every town and city has a hospital. And doctors."

"But not *your* doctor."

She huffed out a breath. “I don’t want to fight with you, Cooper, but let’s get something straight since you still haven’t gotten it through your thick skull. You are not the boss of me. You can’t tell me what to do, especially when it comes to my job. Or my body.” She added that last under her breath but he heard it all the same.

“They’re my babies too, Britt. Why is it so terrible that I want to keep you and them safe?” He caught her face in his hands, and she met his gaze. “I love you. The idea of you being out there somewhere I can’t get to you, of you getting hurt—or worse? It makes me crazy.”

Her expression softened only a tiny bit, her insistent anger still riding just beneath the surface of her emotions.

“You make *me* crazy, Coop.” Her hands circled his wrists, and she pulled his hands away. “Just because I’m carrying babies and my body is a hormonal stew doesn’t make me less than what I’ve always been.”

“I never said that, Britt,” he answered hotly. “Not once. It has nothing to do with your abilities or your intelligence. But it’s not just about you anymore. There are two other lives depending on you. Three, if you include me. I want to marry you. I want you to be my wife. I want to raise our babies together and have more of them whenever you’re ready. Why does that make me the villain in all this?”

“This isn’t about you or what you want,” she spat out, her anger in full bloom now.

His phone chose that inopportune time to ring. Fishing it out of his hip pocket, he answered. Several four-letter words knocked around on his tongue, wanting to be let loose as he listened to the caller. He swallowed the curses, but when he spoke, his voice also held a bit of anger.

"Someone else can deal with this." He listened again, noting Britt's retreat. She curled her upper lip in a snarl and mouthed, "We're done." Then she turned on her heel and marched in the direction of the master bedroom. If he was lucky, she'd lay down with her feet propped up. If he wasn't, he'd find her packing all the clothing that had migrated into his closet.

Cooper went looking for her after he finished the call. He found her in the shower. He hoped that boded well for him and his side of the argument. He tapped on the bathroom door and raised his voice to be heard over the running water. "I have to go deal with a situation on one of the rigs. I'll be gone a couple of hours."

Time enough for her to think things through and maybe see his side of the situation. He got no response. "Will you…" He stopped, biting back what he wanted to say—*will you be here when I get home?* His next thought wasn't much better but he asked anyway. "Will you be okay while I'm gone?"

A strangled noise erupted from the shower stall. It sort of sounded like *argh*, but far more growly. He backed out of the room, realizing he'd pushed his luck way too far. He'd give her time and space, though not too much of either. He wanted to marry her before their babies made their way into the world. He was old-fashioned that way. His parents had been married when his oldest brother Hunter was born. No one believed the family story that Katherine Tate got pregnant on her honeymoon with

Denver and that Hunter was born prematurely. It had been the '70s. And condoms did break. He had personal experience with that particular mishap.

When he first found out Britt was pregnant and he was probably the father, he'd been royally pissed off. That Susie Maddox was alleging the same thing when he knew damn well it wasn't true, just made matters worse. Still, something inside him just...*knew.* Britt was the one he wanted. Stupid Tate curse.

Now, as Cooper drove down the long drive and waited for the electric gate to open, he glanced in the rearview mirror and wondered if Britt would be waiting when he returned.

Britt considered staying in the shower until the hot water ran out. Then she remembered the house had a tankless water heater. She could be in there all day. Glancing at her Swiss Army watch, she figured twenty minutes was long enough. That call had sounded urgent. For Cooper to back out of an argument, it had to be. She turned off the water and listened intently. Silence. Snaking out a hand, she clutched the huge cotton bath sheet hanging next to the shower and wrapped up in it.

She stood alone in the bathroom. So far, so good. On tiptoes, she headed to the bedroom and peeked around the doorjamb. No Cooper. Letting out a relieved sigh, she dried off, brushed her wet hair into a ponytail and dressed. These days, her outfits mostly consisted of stretchy yoga pants and an oversized T-shirt. In the closet, Britt had a large roller bag open and partially packed before she realized that not only did the T-shirt she wore but over half of those she'd packed belonged to Cooper. If she could have bent over, she would have banged her forehead on the top of the built-in dresser.

"Tough," she muttered. She liked his T-shirts. That's why they'd migrated from his drawers into hers. She wouldn't think about the possessive—and totally disarming—grin Cooper wore whenever he caught her wearing his clothes.

She called him a few names in her head. Definitely time for her to get out of here and reclaim her life. Bossy man. Trying to tell her what to do, and when and how she could do it.

Pregnancy did not affect her ability to work. Everyone comprehended that except Cooper. Old-fashioned jerk. Speaking of which, they didn't have to be married to parent the twins. That was the other thing they argued about. A lot. She could manage as a single mother. Even with twins. He'd pay her child support. Heck, he'd already put her on his insurance, much to the happiness of Channel 2's human resources lady. He'd also paid all her deductibles and out-of-pocket expenses. He'd pay for day care, whether he liked it or not. He was such a chauvinist that he probably expected her to stay home and take care of his house and kids.

That thought brought her up short. No, she had to be honest. He had never once said that. He also didn't oppose her working as long as it was at the station. Indoors. Where it was safe. And he'd never said anything about her stopping storm chasing after the twins arrived and her maternity leave was over.

She rubbed her eyes with the heels of her hands because they were stinging all of a sudden. Cooper didn't object to her storm chasing. He just didn't want her to do it while she was pregnant. They'd never discussed her staying home or going back to work after the twins were born. He'd suggested she take some time to finish her doctoral dissertation, submit it, and finally get her PhD. She realized in that moment that, in his way, he supported what she did. And she did want those initials before and after her name. Dr. Brittney Owens, PhD, Meteorology.

Something soft brushed against her calf and she jumped. "Dang, Lucifer," she growled. "Don't do that."

The scruffy cat stared up at her, his gaze reproving. Why couldn't Cooper be a dog person? Something big and goofy. A Bloodhound maybe. Or a Newfoundland like Harley. Harley was a cool dog. Lucifer? He just had a bad attitude, sharp teeth and claws, and didn't like anybody but Cooper. And she wasn't totally sure the cat actually liked Cooper.

Conceding the staring contest to the cat, she glanced around the closet. How had so many of her clothes ended up here? It wasn't like she'd officially moved in with him or anything. Was she the only one denying that's what it really was?

He'd tried to convince her. And it was easy to let the charm of the place win her over. Though the house was surrounded by city—the view of downtown Oklahoma City was spectacular at night as they sat on the covered deck—the place was insulated by several acres of pasture and trees. A historic home, the inside was updated and while mostly masculine, it felt homey and comfortable. Too comfortable. Yes, definitely time to go home. To stay. She'd make arrangements to get the rest of her clothes later.

She hoisted the suitcase onto the floor and froze as her lower back twinged. Lucifer's expression implied a very feline, "I told you so." She curled her lip in an answering snarl. "I'm fine." But she did make a note to self to not lift the suitcase. Which meant getting it into and out of her truck would be problematic.

The cat trailed her to the front door. Britt set the alarm, let herself out, and locked the door using the electronic keypad. In the short time she'd been with Cooper—

"No!" she corrected herself. "We aren't together. Not *together*. Just…together. I'm not living here." Except she'd left a boatload of clothes behind. She'd come back to get them later. Because she was so done with this. He didn't trust her to be smart when it came to the twins and there was no way she could be with a man who dismissed her like that.

"We aren't a couple," she reminded herself. "We aren't even friends."

Nope, definitely not friends. They fought too much, but there were amazing benefits. The sexual chemistry between them was freaking amazing. And he didn't mind that she basically had a beach ball strapped to her middle. Cooper found inventive ways to get both of them off.

Nope, definitely couldn't think about that. If Cooper got his way, he'd walk all over her. She had a life to live and she was better off without him. That was her story and she was sticking to it.

Seventeen

Two weeks. It had been two weeks since Britt had left. She wouldn't accept his calls. Blocked his texts. Stubborn woman. Half her clothes remained in his closet. He had been petty enough to have Bridger set up codes in the alarm system so he'd get an alert if she sneaked into the house to retrieve the rest of her stuff. He could be just as stubborn as her.

He was almost desperate enough to do something drastic—like have Chance file the court papers to ensure he got joint custody when the twins arrived. And he was doing everything he could to keep his temper in check.

But this morning, when Bridger walked through his office door, his brother's announcement blew the lid off.

"We need to talk about Britt, Coop."

His fist slammed the wall two inches from Bridger's face. "I'm not falling into that trap."

"Dude, you aren't falling, you're running full steam ahead into it. It's not a matter of the family interfering, it's a matter of you recognizing how messed up this is."

Cooper rubbed the back of his neck with the hand free of bleeding knuckles, breathing around the knot of anger cinching his chest. Bridger was right. This whole thing was out of control and his brain was right there circling the drain of chaos.

"She is the mother of my babies," he argued. "I have a duty to her."

"What about a duty to yourself? Do you really want to tie yourself down to a woman who wants nothing to do with you? A woman who could be using you, and is probably lying to you?"

"She has no reason to lie. She didn't even know the condom broke. And the timing is exactly right. I'm the only man she's been with."

"Be honest with yourself, Coop. You're not worried about falling for a lie when the real problem is that you're falling in love with a woman you can't trust." Sympathy suffused Bridger's face. "Let the past be a lesson, big bro. Just look at Hunter."

The reminder of their oldest brother's experience was a bucket of ice water dumped over his head. Hunter had fallen for the wrong woman and when she betrayed him, he'd shut down emotionally. The whole family still lived with the fallout and it had been years.

He continued staring at his feet, thinking. He didn't owe Britt anything, especially since she refused to have anything to do with him. But Bridger was right. He had fallen for her. His anger ebbed slightly. "When did you get to be so smart, little bro?"

His brother walked away, getting in the last word as he often did. "I'll get some ice for that hand."

When Bridger returned with a chemical ice pack, he got the first word in too. "I'm the smart one. I learned from all the screw-ups my older brothers made. Being next to the youngest helps. Y'all made the mistakes. I took notes."

Cooper would have wiped the smirk off Bridge's face but his right hand still throbbed from almost putting his fist through the wall earlier. He leaned his head back against the couch, eyes closed, hand throbbing. He'd probably broken something. He hoped the ice pack helped.

"Can I be honest?"

He opened one eye to look at his little brother. "If I tell you to shut up, will you?"

"Nope."

He closed his eye. "Fine. Go for it."

"Does it matter?"

"What's that supposed to mean?"

"You barely know this woman, Coop." Bridge held up a hand. "Yes, she's been staying at your house but it's not like y'all have anything in common. At least consider a prenuptial if you ever get her to marry you. Otherwise, your life might end up in the toilet."

That got him up and moving, both eyes open, a scowl on his face. "I don't need a prenup. And it's my life, Bridger."

"She doesn't want you."

"She's having my twins."

"So what? She's done everything possible to keep you out of her life. Why are you so stubborn?"

"What part of *she's having my twins* do you not understand?"

"Has it occurred to you that this might be part of some plan to trap you? That she's figured out if she runs fast enough, you'll chase her until she catches you?"

"She's not like that."

"Says the man so desperate to marry the woman he's lost all common sense."

"It matters, Bridger. That's all there is to it."

His cell phone rang. He ignored it. A minute after it stopped ringing, the intercom on his desk buzzed. He ignored it too. Two minutes later, Nikki knocked twice and stuck her head through the door before he could tell her to go away.

"You need to answer your phone, boss. Your little brother is slightly hysterical."

Coop exchanged a look with Bridger. "Little brother? Which one?"

"Tucker. Something to do with Zoe and Britt."

His cell rang again and he snagged it. "Tuck?"

"What the hell, Coop? Your idiot girlfriend has dragged Zoe out in that monster truck of hers."

"Wait. What?"

"Storm chasing, Cooper. I got home and found a note from Zoe. She's with Britt and they've gone storm chasing!"

* * *

Britt pulled off to the side of the road to check her computer. Zoe was wide-eyed and all but bouncing up and down in the back seat. Leo rolled his eyes though Britt figured he was a little awed by their VIP passenger. The big teddy bear was a fan. She looked out through the windshield. A massive shelf cloud swirled around the bottom of a classic anvil formation. It was just a matter of time before a supercell storm formed.

Leo was on the phone with the station. Dave was periodically going live with updates and the station would be taking her shot soon. Everything was ready.

Zoe leaned up between the bucket seats. "I promise to be quiet when you go on the air. I'm just so excited that you called me and that Tucker and I were in town so I could come out and play with you. I've been tellin' everyone in Nashville that I was gonna get to go storm chasin' with you. They're all jealous."

Laughing, Britt said, "If this storm turns into a supercell, and it's showing every indication that it will, you'll definitely have something to talk about."

The next few hours were a whirlwind of driving, heavy rain, gusty winds, back roads and that big storm building to gigantic proportions. The Gentner crackled with communications among the various chase teams. Britt and Leo were both on their cell phones and Zoe was taking pictures with her smartphone and posting them on Instagram. Britt watched the storm front; Leo watched the GPS mapping system installed in the truck.

"Britt, we're getting into ranch country. That means closed sections and maybe running out of road."

"We'll be fine. I have a feeling this sucker is going to drop a big one, Leo. We need to be right there when it does."

Something *pinged* on the roof of the truck. More pings. Britt kept driving while talking to Dave on the air.

"There's a massive hail core with this storm, Britt," Dave said. "And it looks like you are right on the edge of it."

"We are, Dave. It started off with pea-sized hail and now we're experiencing quarter size. No, wait. Do you have Leo's shot up? That's golf-ball size and it's really pounding the truck."

A voice buzzed in her ear. Ria. "Britt, there's some serious rotation cranking up to your southwest. Can you move that way? It will get you out of the hail core and radar is showing winds gusting up to sixty in the area of rotation. If there's an updraft—"

Britt cut her off. "We're on it."

She didn't bother trying to turn around. They were the only vehicle on this section line road so she just threw the transmission into Reverse and backed up until they hit the next crossroad. Turning around, she headed south until they could get a road headed to the west. That's when she got her first good look at the storm's presentation. A massive supercell complex of clouds looking for all the world like a gigantic spaceship hovered over the plains of western Oklahoma. The entire base was rotating and rain fell in cascades at its center. The inflow and updraft were apparent.

"Holy cow, Leo. Please tell me this is streaming live."

Dave's voice came over the Gentner. "You're live on the station's app as well as live here in the studio, Britt. This storm is every bit as dangerous as both the EF-4 and EF-5 Moore tornadoes. People need to take their tornado precautions immediately. Get underground. If you live in—" Dave named off all the towns in the storm's path, but Britt was too busy to pay attention. She had radar up on her laptop, with one eye on the screen and the other on the storm. She'd studied the long-track storms that often hit Oklahoma and this monster looked just like them.

Excitement built, fueled by adrenaline. She'd stopped on a hill and could see all the way from the Wichita Mountains down by Lawton to almost the Oklahoma City metro area. There was a lot of territory to cover before this storm hit the city but she'd bet money that it would track close.

A wind gust rocked the truck and she checked her instruments. "Ria," she said into the Bluetooth receiver pinned to her shirt. "We just got hit with eighty-mile-per-hour outflow. I can feel it. This supercell is going to start dropping tornadoes any minute now." And then Zoe was squealing, Leo adjusting the cameras, and Britt was yelling into the microphone. "Tornadoes on the ground, Dave. We have multiple tornadoes on the ground."

Eighteen

Cooper stood on the brakes and his big truck skidded to a stop in the travel center's parking lot. His heart pounded in his chest like a jackhammer and he could barely breathe. It took effort to peel his fingers off the steering wheel. Tucker was already out of the passenger door and sprinting toward Britt's chase vehicle. When he jumped down, he slammed the door so hard the truck rocked.

By the time he arrived, Britt and Zoe were chattering excitedly. His brother glared at Britt while his hands checked his wife. Tuck visibly relaxed as Zoe's words penetrated.

"Lordy be! That was the most excitement I've had in ages. I mean, I haven't been in a car goin' that fast since that time in Knoxville when the Smithees came after us." Zoe turned her face to her husband, eyes dancing and face beaming. "You remember that time, darlin', right? I almost ran you down in the Volunteermobile."

Coop had heard that story and it had nothing to do with now. Britt looked every bit as excited as Zoe. Emotions so intense he could neither name them nor have any chance of controlling them surged up. Before he could stop to think, he grabbed Britt's shoulder and spun her around. His hands reached for her and he gripped her biceps. As much as he wanted to shake her, he held her carefully. Too bad he couldn't control his voice with the same care. His question came out as a shout. "What is wrong with you?"

She flinched and he clamped an iron fist on his roiling anger. No, not anger. At least not completely. No. This was beyond anger. Fear. It was unadulterated terror that took his heart and lungs captive so that he couldn't breathe, could barely think. He had his hands on her, could see she was alive and standing here, acting for all the world like she'd been on some wildly fun carnival ride. He didn't know whether to kiss her or kill her, because she'd come far too close to death as it was.

"Look at me," he yelled when she wouldn't meet his glare. "What were you thinking?" He bent closer to her so they stood eye-to-eye. "Oh, wait. You weren't thinking."

She pulled against his hold, her anger splashing her cheeks with bright pink. "I was doing my job."

"Your job? Where in your bloody job description does it say you have to be so damn close to a storm that you have to run for your life when it drops a tornado on top of you?"

"I'm fine." Britt spat the words from between gritted teeth.

"You could have died." The words tore out of him, wrenched from the very depths of everything he felt for this woman, for who and what she was to him.

She rolled her eyes and huffed out an aggrieved sigh. "But I didn't."

"No, by the grace of God you didn't. Did you stop to think what would happen if Zoe got hurt by your stupidity?"

"My what?" She arched up like an angry cat and all but spit at him. "I'm not stupid, Cooper. I was paying attention. But sometimes, spin-ups like that happen in places where they shouldn't. It happens all the time."

"Spin-ups? That wasn't a spin-up, Britt. That was a freaking F-3 tornado. And it chased you. For miles. I watched. Because you were live streaming the whole damn thing. Was getting views and likes more important than your safety? Than Zoe's?"

"Of course not. We're fine, Cooper. Zoe has an awesome story to tell when she's interviewed. Leo got amazing footage."

"Nope." The normally affable cameraman held up his hands and backed away from the little group. "You leave me out of this because you know what? I happen to agree with Cooper, Britt. Given those roads and the way that storm was spinning, the gust front that built up? I may not be a degreed meteorologist like you, girl, but I've done my share of watching from the co-pilot's seat. We should not have been that close."

Britt's lip curled up in a snarl and her nose crinkled. Once upon a time, Cooper might have thought her expression cute. Now? Now it just caused his anger to boil over. Before he could speak, she turned on Leo.

"Thanks a lot, Leo. I thought you were a team player. Good to know that you believe I can't do my job. I'll let the station know you won't be riding with me anymore. In fact, you better just call them right now to get a ride because I'm done with you. I know what I'm doing. I'm good at what I do. Stuff happens. It happened today. But I got us away. Because. I. Know. My. Job."

She stepped back from Tucker and jerked hard. He let her go because to hang on would mean tightening his grip and he didn't want to hurt her. He was so mad he wanted to hit something, but it wouldn't be Britt. Cooper glanced around. Tucker had Zoe snugged up close to his side and Coop recognized the dawning realization in her expression. Leo just looked disgusted with the whole thing.

"I'm fine. We're all fine. Whether anyone wants to admit that or not. You know what. I'm done with this. That storm is still out there. My truck is running fine and I'm going back out." She jabbed a finger at Leo. "With or without you." Then she whirled to Cooper. "And you don't have a say in this. We're done."

Britt stood there breathing fire like she had a reason to be angry at him. She might be done, but he wasn't. "We aren't done, Britt. I have every right to—"

"You have no rights, Cooper." She threw up her hands. "I'm so outta here."

He clenched his fists to keep from reaching for her. "You're having my babies, Britt."

She grimaced, eyes narrowed, cheeks flushed, hands on her hips. She had to loosen her jaw to speak. "Trust me, I'm totally freaking aware of that."

He pointed to her truck. The back seat window on the driver's side was cracked. The hood was peppered with dents from the hailstorm they'd been caught in. The tailgate had a huge gouge where a piece of debris, driven by tornado-force winds, had slammed into it. "You. Could. Have. Died. And killed my children. *Our* babies." His voice dropped and he leaned toward her again. "Zoe was in that vehicle with you. My sister-in-law. The love of my brother's life, the mother of his little boy. And Leo. Your friend and colleague. He has a family too. But even if they weren't there, even if it was just you in that truck, you. Could. Have. Died. You, Britt."

Britt inhaled and he braced for another one of her tirades—about how it was her job, about how she was perfectly capable, about all the total bullshit she'd spouted at him for the past six months. But he beat her to the punch.

"I sat there, watching that damn tornado running up your tailpipe, Britt. Praying you got away. Knowing there was no way in hell you could. And I knew." He thumped a fist against his chest over his heart. "I knew right here that I was going to lose it all. You. Our babies." The breath he sucked in sent shudders through his body. "You wanna know what was going through my head?"

She blinked up at him, wide-eyed, the rosy color draining from her face. "What?" she whispered.

"Picking out your coffin. Buying a burial plot. Music. Flowers. All the stuff that goes with planning a funeral instead of a wedding and a honeymoon." He had to stop, to blink the sting from his eyes because he wanted to see her face, wanted to see her expression. "I faced my worst nightmare, Britt. I sat there thinking that I would have to bury you and our babies before I ever got the chance to meet them. To love them. To love you. Except I already do."

Someone sniffled but it wasn't Britt. Probably Zoe. And knowing Zoe, the woman would most likely turn this whole fiasco into a song. He stared at Britt. She stared back. Her blank expression shouldn't have surprised him. She was so determined to prove that she was always right, that she could do everything all on her own. What she didn't understand was that he admired her. He thought she was a little crazy, but he respected her intelligence and her drive. But she was having *his* babies and being reckless was no longer an option. When she gave him no response, he turned to walk away but paused for one last comment.

"Losing you? Losing them? I'm not sure I could survive that."

Britt stood there in shocked silence, her anger melting away into…something she didn't quite recognize. Remorse? Maybe. She was a woman in a man's field and she constantly fought for every scrap, standing up for herself, asserting her independence and abilities. And then she'd gotten pregnant. By a man with old-fashioned values. A man who understood responsibility and was willing to step up and accept his. He was also overbearing and irritating and pushy and if she wasn't careful, she'd hand him her heart and he could crush it so easily. Just like she'd crushed his.

I sat there thinking that I would have to bury you and our babies before I ever got the chance to meet them. To love them. To love you. Except I already do.

Those words had seared her ears and burned their way into her brain. *To love them. To love you.* Did he mean that? He'd told her that more than once and she just blew him off for trying to manipulate her. She closed her eyes, fought the urge to rub them because she knew she was perilously close to crying. *Except I already do.* What did he mean by that? That he loved the twins? That he loved…*her*? That couldn't be. He didn't know her. Not really. Oh sure, they'd shared a bed, lived in the same house. Had sexual chemistry hot enough to set off a four-alarm fire. But how could he love her?

Losing you? Losing them? I'm not sure I could survive that. She'd started to scoff but then the force of his emotions slammed her like hundred-mile-an-hour straight winds. He meant every word. He loved her. Loved their babies. And losing them? That would be the end of his world. And she knew that feeling so freaking well because their babies meant everything to her too.

She opened her eyes to realize that Cooper was walking away. Leo stood near her truck looking aggravated and disgusted. Tucker and Zoe stood in a tight embrace, their faces hidden. Her vision blurred as understanding washed over her.

"You're right. I'm sorry."

She saw that her soft admission shocked Cooper when he turned around, brows raised, mouth slightly opening as his jaw dropped.

"What did you say?" His voice was whisper quiet but held a hard edge, like he didn't quite believe her.

"I said that you're right and that I'm sorry."

Cooper pushed a booted foot forward as if he was stepping toward her but then halted, frozen in place. His arms hung limp at his sides and his expression held both confusion and despair. And yeah, he was still angry. She supposed he had a right to hang onto some of his mad. Most of all, though, she could see the fear and hopelessness. She remembered that look on her father's face when her little brother had been hit by a car. He was in a coma for three days and her dad kept a constant vigil before Bruce came out of it. Her mother had been long gone by then.

Britt had adored her dad and appreciated everything he'd given up to raise her and her brother. He'd never remarried after the divorce and died while she was in college. She and her brother drifted apart and she was a bit jealous of the close family ties Cooper had. Still, if a single man could raise two kids, she could raise the twins. She wasn't going to be like her mother. No way.

But what if her mother had taken her away when she abandoned the family? It would have killed her dad.

And seeing that same look on Cooper's face now? Yeah, she had to fix this.

If Cooper wasn't going to come to her, she'd have to go to him. She supposed it was about time because truthfully? He'd always been the one to reach out to her and she'd swatted him away each time. No wonder he was a little gun-shy.

She took the first step toward him. Then the second. Slow. Easy. Like she was approaching a scared dog. She almost smiled as she thought the words, "Easy, boy." But she didn't. Cooper wouldn't understand a smile at this point. She stopped in front of him. Slowly, she raised her hand and brushed her fingers along his jawline, her eyes glued to his. Deep blue, his eyes. All the Tate brothers had blue eyes but Cooper's were a blue that reminded her of the twilight sky.

"I'm sorry, Cooper. I'm sorry I yelled. I'm sorry I took chances. I'm sorry I scared you."

His hand captured hers so fast she gasped. He raised her fingertips to his mouth and he kissed each one before lowering their hands to his chest. He pressed her palm over his heart. The thump-thump-thump beat against her hand, slightly erratic like he'd been running, but strong and true. Just like the man.

"Feel that, Girl Wonder?"

She nodded.

"That's what you do to me."

A surprised smile tugged at one corner of her mouth and she felt her expression soften with no effort on her part. "Good to know," she murmured, looking away.

His arm curled around her back and she looked up

at him. Now it was her heart's turn to beat erratically. This man…he undid her. She wanted to kiss his full lips, to lean into his warmth and find shelter there. And then he spoke.

"Marry me."

Again, it came down to the line she couldn't cross, the leap she couldn't take. She'd caught a brief glimpse of his fear, his vulnerability, maybe even his love for her. But were they really any closer to seeing eye-to-eye, or would they go back to bickering once the crisis blew over?

"I'm sorry, Coop." She backed away from him and all but ran to her truck. She leaned on the hood and called, "I just can't."

Nineteen

Coop stared out the window of his office and considered his options. He had to admit that maybe he shouldn't have mentioned marriage right when Britt was admitting she'd messed up, one, by taking Zoe storm chasing, and two, by getting too close to that supercell. She'd stormed off, pun totally intended, because all he had left was a warped sense of humor.

Someone cleared their throat and he glanced at the reflection of his office in the glass, surprised to find his boss's wife there. "Jolie?"

"Cooper."

He turned to face her and discovered compassion rather than censure in her expression. "Let's hope you haven't totally mucked this up."

"I probably have."

"You know what Cord and I went through. I left town without telling him I was pregnant. I even managed to get through nursing clinicals while I was pregnant. I also raised CJ as a single mom until he was four." She flashed him a wry smile. "Not the brightest thing I ever did, but I managed. What I've seen of Britt, she can pretty much do whatever she wants. You need to remember that. Pregnancy isn't a handicap."

He turned back to the view outside his window and leaned his forehead against the glass. He knew that. But Britt's job—what she did when storm watches were issued—could be dangerous. And she was carrying twins. *His* twins. He loved her and wanted her safe. Wanted their babies safe. No one would believe him if he admitted that he awoke in the middle of the night, heart pounding, breath caught in his chest. His nightmare? That Britt was out in the middle of nowhere, a tornado bearing down on her while she was in labor and he couldn't get to her. Just like two weeks ago.

"She scares me," he admitted, his voice hoarse.

"No. What she *does* scares you. Y'all need to work through this, Coop." Jolie came up behind him and slipped her arms around his waist for a loose hug. "I've got faith in you. If the Bee Dubyas can help, all you gotta do is holler."

He patted her hands where they rested on his abdomen. "I know. And it's appreciated."

Jolie slipped out of his office as quietly as she'd come in, leaving him alone with plenty of time to think. As long as Britt was at his house, he knew where she was. As long as she was at the station, he knew where she was. As long as she was with him, he knew where she was. His brothers said he was crazy. Except maybe for Tucker and Deacon. They had wives and kids. They'd get it.

It had been two weeks. Britt had reverted to refusing his calls and texts so he'd stopped after the first couple of days. And she'd been storm chasing. He almost couldn't watch Channel 2 when the weather turned bad. Which was turning out to be almost every day. Thunderstorms with torrential rains leading to flooding. Thunderstorms with hail ranging from quarter- to baseball-sized. Thunderstorms with high winds and tornadoes. And Britt was out there, confronting the storms and relaying information back to the station.

She was out there. Day and night. Dark circles were constantly present beneath her eyes when he caught her on-screen. It was like Britt had to prove herself, over and over. Which wasn't true. Cooper discussed things with Tucker. Both the station manager and head meteorologist would happily make a spot for her on air in the studio but she was such an adrenaline junkie she refused every offer.

His cell phone pinged from where it sat on his desk. He glanced over. A weather alert. Great. He debated deleting the app, knew he wouldn't. Ever. Because Britt would always be out there in it, facing danger. Picking up the phone, he read through the warning. Severe storms, yada yada. He flipped to the radar portion of the app and hit his intercom.

"Nikki, you watchin' the weather?"

"Yessir. I have radar up on my computer. I'm in the process of calling our people now."

Coop let out a half laugh. "Why do I even bother?"

"Well, in that case, how about a raise?"

"Don't push your luck, Nickelodeon."

"Can't blame a girl for trying, bossman." She chuckled and muttered, "There's always diamonds."

He clicked off and returned to the windows, circling around for a different view. From this angle, he could see the front moving in from the southwest. Something twisted in his gut. This was going to be a bad one and Britt would be right in the middle of the storm. There was no way he could sit still. He grabbed his phone and headed out.

"I'm going to check on the rigs. Send the staff home early."

"But—"

"Tell Cord to check radar. This storm is shaping up just like those monster Moore tornadoes. Nobody needs to be caught out on the highway."

"Says the man who's going toward the storm."

He ignored her and headed toward the elevator.

Britt awoke that morning feeling out of sorts. So what else was new? Even Ria was put out with her. Leo refused to get in the truck with her until she got her temper under control. She'd argued that she didn't have a temper, while promptly losing it. Men! They were good for opening pickle jars, reaching stuff on the top shelf and zipping up dresses. Nothing else.

She stayed in the shower for longer than normal. Her

back ached—so what else was new with two potential soccer stars in her womb. She was angry. Two weeks. And he hadn't come after her. But he totally loved her and the babies. *Right.*

Okay, to be honest, she *had* walked out on him without a word. He'd tried to talk to her but she hadn't responded. Nor had she accepted his calls. And she wasn't one of those women who played games. Yet here she was doing just that. What was wrong with her? She rubbed the side of her belly where one of the terrible twosome had just hit her with a roundhouse kick. "Swear to God I'm gonna name you guys Chuck and Norris."

The babies settled a bit. Distraction over, her thoughts returned to her very complicated relationship with Cooper. She truly hadn't left with the intent of him following to beg her to stay. But he'd been so persistent in his pursuit. Why would he suddenly stop? Had he found someone else? Someone skinny and beautiful? Or sweet? All three of those criteria could be met by ninety-nine percent of the female population of Oklahoma City and surrounding environs.

Coming out of the shower, she'd found her phone blown up with texts, missed calls and several voice mails. She listened to those while reading her messages. Great. A big storm front with all the signs of producing multiple supercell thunderstorms was amassed in the southwestern part of the state, moving northeast toward the metro area. The skin on the back of her neck prickled as goose bumps rose on her skin. She didn't believe in psychic stuff but she had a bad feeling about this storm.

Mind made up, she loaded up her truck to head toward the station. If Leo wouldn't ride with her, she'd coerce one of the other photojournalists.

Driving northbound on the interstate, she still had a funny feeling in her stomach, sort of a cross between butterflies and a stomachache from too much sweet stuff. And she was still angry at Cooper. She really needed to get over that. But the farther north she drove, the madder she got. If she took the back way to the station, she could drive by Cooper's house. If he was there, she could stop and give him a piece of her mind.

The longer she thought about it, the more it seemed like an excellent idea. She could tell him what she really thought about him.

A sharp pain stabbed her in the lower back and she felt a gush between her legs. She managed to steer the truck to the side of the highway. A growing red splotch stained the hem of the light blue maternity T-shirt she wore. Nausea racked her body and she managed to find a plastic bag. Light-headed, sick and in pain, she groped blindly for her phone and hit the first number on her favorites list.

Three rings. Four. "Pickuppickuppickup," she chanted, terrified she'd pass out—or worse.

"What?"

"Something's wrong."

Every nightmare he'd ever had about Britt and her pregnancy froze Cooper in place as he stepped off the elevator in the parking garage and heard her voice. "Where are you?"

"I… I'm…" Her voice faded and he was terrified that she was out in the middle of nowhere, that she might lose cell phone reception. "I-35. Um…"

"Baby, you gotta talk to me."

"Northbound. South of I-40."

He ran toward his truck. "Have you passed the Shields Boulevard exit?"

"I… I don't know."

"Britt, talk to me. What's happening?"

"I… I'm not sure. There's… I hurt. And I can't think. There's blood." Her voice caught then she sobbed out, "There's blood, Cooper. I'm scared."

He didn't stop to think. He just jumped in his truck and tore out of the Barron Tower's parking garage. He had enough presence of mind to put the phone on Bluetooth so he could drive with both hands. "I'm comin' that way, sweet girl. Just hang on. Keep talking to me."

"Coop…"

"I'm here, darlin'. I'm here."

"Something's wrong with the babies. I… This morning… I was all… I don't know. Feeling weird. And my back hurt. Down low. I took a hot shower. I was so mad at you."

"Mad at me?" He tried to keep his voice light and teasing. "What'd I do now?"

"You weren't here. And you don't believe in me."

He laughed but it sounded bitter, because he was. "I believe in you, Britt. I just want you and our babies safe. Is that so terrible?"

His damn pride—and fear. If not for that, he would have been with her when this happened. He wouldn't be driving like a maniac trying to locate her.

"No. But you could have talked to me instead of getting all bossy." Her voice sounded very small and unsure and that was not Britt. She was a confident woman full of life and energy. Salt and vinegar, his mother called it.

"Yeah, Girl Wonder, I could have. Wanna know a secret? I've been miserable without you."

"Good."

He had to smile at her snippy voice. That was so much better than before. She'd sounded so…lost.

"I'm comin' now, Britt. And I won't ever let you walk away again."

"Promise?" She sounded lost again and his heart broke a little bit more.

"Cross my heart."

Navigating downtown streets, road construction, and the weird loop to get on I-40 and southbound on I-35 took all his concentration. He didn't talk. Neither did Britt. He listened to her breathing, noting each change, and fought the panic welling deep inside him. With the impending storm, traffic was thick but police were scarce. He drove his truck like it was an Indy race car while scanning the northbound shoulder for any sign of Britt's storm chaser vehicle. It would be easy to spot.

He found her just north of Northeast 27th Street in Moore. He used the exits and on-ramps to execute a U-turn. He pulled up behind her, jumped out and ran to the driver's side door, jerking it open. Britt all but fell into his arms, sobbing. Blood pooled in the seat beneath her.

"Are you having contractions?"

"No."

He should call 9-1-1. He didn't. He grabbed her backpack and locked her vehicle. Cradling her in his arms, he loped back to his truck, strapped Britt into the passenger seat, and jumped in behind the wheel. They were less than three miles away from a satellite hospital with a Level II trauma center. He called Britt's doctor first. Then he called his mother. He briefed her quickly, his attention ping-ponging from their conversation, to Britt, to traffic, to the dark line of clouds he could see out the windshield.

Cooper finished up. "Gotta go. We're here. Stay at the ranch, Mom. Weather's getting worse. I'll keep you posted."

He stomped the brake pedal and the truck skidded to a stop next to the emergency room entrance. He was out and easing Britt into his arms when a security guard appeared.

"Never mind. Move the truck later," the man directed as soon as he assessed the situation.

A nurse met them in the reception area, leading them straight back, chattering instructions as they went. Most of the information went straight over Cooper's head. Passing through an interior waiting area, Coop glanced at the TV mounted to the wall. Dave Edmonds was onscreen, pointing to huge splotches of brilliant red on the radar image behind him. The sound was turned up.

"Ria," Dave was saying. "Where's Britt? Is she on the Gentner yet?"

He'd have to call the station. Someone would notice Britt's empty truck sooner or later. He laid her on an exam table and stepped back, but not out of the room, as the nurse shooed him away. More calls—one to Channel 2, and one to Bridger to deal with Britt's vehicle—all the while also listening to the nurse and then the doctor—ER, not OBGYN—who came jogging in.

Ten minutes later, following an exam and ultrasound, they were watching a live stream of KOCX's weather on Coop's phone because Britt wouldn't settle and all the medical personnel kept fussing at her to relax to bring her blood pressure down. Coop sat on a rolling stool, arm propped on the exam table, holding the phone so they both could watch.

The live footage was terrifying, invoking memories of the historic F-5 tornadoes on May 3, 1999 and May 20, 2013. A massive funnel churned across the landscape devouring everything in its path. Dr. Morgan, Britt's OB, arrived and paused to watch. Then she turned to Britt.

"Decision time. The good news is, the twins should be fine, we've got equipment here and a pediatrician is on-call, just in case. Bad news is, we need to get them born ASAP." She rolled right over Cooper's question and Britt's denial. "The choice you need to make, young lady, is whether to induce labor or go with a C-section. If we induce, we might still have to do the C-section if they go into worse distress."

Her eyes found his and he knew what his decision

would be. The C-section. Get them out and to medical help immediately. But it was her body. He shrugged. "Up to you, Britt."

One of her hands stroked the mound of her belly. The other squeezed his arm. "How soon can you do the C-section if nature doesn't work?"

"We can prep you now and do it as soon as the pediatrician gets here. Anesthesiologist is in the building. OR nurses are prepping the room. You've begun to dilate, and we've started the Pitocin drip. We'll know shortly if that works."

Britt inhaled and held it as she watched the news feed for several moments, reading the radar. Then she exhaled. "That's what we'll do then. Tell the baby doctor to get here fast. We need to get this show on the road."

Twenty

The drugs kicked in before they got Britt moved to the operating room. Cooper had no idea she could heap so many curses upon him, the doctors and nurses, and the world in general. The doctor just chuckled and muttered that Pitocin hit some women like a race car going from zero to 100 in 3.2 seconds. Britt went from barely dilated and no contractions to having hard contractions two minutes apart. Too late for Lamaze classes so he was winging it, and trying to keep her occupied by watching the live footage of the impending storm.

Britt snatched his phone and stared at the radar presentation. "No-no-no," she murmured.

"I need current data." She glanced up at him and, as another contraction hit, gritted out, "I need a TV. I need the live feed."

The nurse gave her an odd look so Cooper explained. “She’s a meteorologist at KOCX.”

The nurse’s eyes widened in surprise. “That’s why you look so familiar! You’re one of the storm chasers.”

Five minutes later, a maintenance man rolled in a cart with a TV. He fiddled with cords and cables and then the screen flared to life. “What channel?” he asked.

“Two,” everyone in the room chorused.

As soon as the channel changed, Britt let out a stream of muttered words that Cooper had no hope of translating. Then he realized she was doing some sort of calculations in her head. She turned to the nurse.

“How many people are here?”

“I’m… I have no idea.”

“What’s your emergency protocol?”

“For storms?”

“Yes.”

“Move everyone to the basement,” the nurse replied.

“Then you need to do that. Now.” Britt doubled up as another contraction hit, but her words had been forcefully calm.

Cooper squeezed her hand. “Britt?”

“It’s on the ground, just like the monsters that hit this area before. Same track, Cooper. People need to be underground. Like…now.”

A woman in a business suit appeared in the doorway. “I’m the hospital administrator One of the nurses said there was a situation.”

“You need to implement your emergency protocols.” Britt cut her off, pointing to the TV. “Unless that sucker decides to collapse, the tornado is going to tear through here."

Edmonds's voice droned in the background. "Radar indicates wind speeds well into the EF4 range. I can't stress enough that any of our viewers in the path of this storm need to get off the roads and get underground. Now."

Britt shuddered through another contraction. "You heard the man. Now."

Controlled chaos ensued. One nurse stayed with Britt while the rest of the staff worked to move patients and visitors into the basement storage area. This meant moving monitoring equipment, IVs, beds. Britt squeezed Cooper's hand. "You need to help."

"No. I need to be here with you."

"Running out of options, Hero Boy. Time to put on your cape."

He didn't want to leave her but he could hear rising voices outside. People were starting to panic. He kissed her, saying, "Don't have those babies until I get back."

Britt rolled her eyes and snorted. "They'll get here when they get here."

Stepping outside the operating room, Coop waded into the pandemonium. Glancing out a window, he understood why. Straight winds of at least eighty miles per hour pushed debris across the parking lot, rocking cars and uprooting trees planted in medians. The wind was so strong, the torrential rain was driven horizontally. He borrowed a few of Britt's more colorful curses to mutter under his breath as he grabbed a hospital bed and helped the nurse guide it onto the elevator.

Ten minutes later, he and the ER doctor cleared the second then the first floors of the hospital. Everyone had been evacuated to the basement. Everyone but Britt, Dr. Morgan and a nurse who volunteered to stay in the OR. The twins were premature. Moving Britt into an unsterile area like the basement for their birth was out of the question. The weather conditions outside continued to deteriorate and as Cooper and the ER doc headed across the lobby, one of the front windows blew out. He pushed the doctor through the interior doors, slammed them shut and dragged furniture in front of them before jogging to the operating room.

As they entered, Cooper realized that Dr. Morgan was at the foot of the operating table, and the only word she said that he understood was, "Push."

"I *am* pushing," Britt yelled.

The lights flickered as Cooper shut the door behind him.

"Don't worry," the nurse called. "We have a backup generator."

Cooper *was* worried. He'd caught the latest radar right before the window shattered. They were in the direct path of the tornado. He shuffled to the head of the bed and grabbed one of Britt's hands as she flailed them. Good thing his ego wasn't fragile. She yelled all sorts of things about him. All of a sudden, she curled up toward her knees and bore down. He slipped an arm around her back to support her.

Two things happened simultaneously—the lights went out and a baby cried louder than the roar of the freight train bearing down on them.

* * *

Bridger stared at the ruins of the hospital. One lone fire truck was there, along with a police car. The tornado had scoured a long path through the southern edge of Oklahoma City and smack dab through the middle of Moore. There weren't enough first responders and too many civilians who didn't know what they were doing or were too shell-shocked to help were clogging the parking lot. Cell phone service was dead—too many cell towers damaged or destroyed and too many people trying to make calls tying up the towers still working. Good thing he had a two-way radio in his SUV. All Barron Security officers and agents had them.

"We're watching the footage," Cash said seconds after Bridge called in. "What do you need?"

"Wreckers, pole trucks, anything that can lift debris or shift rubble. Coop let me know that everyone in the hospital had evacuated to the basement. Except him, a couple of doctors and Britt. She was in active labor."

"The basement isn't the only safe room in that hospital, Bridge."

"I know but the top floor is just…gone. And what's left of the first floor is buried. I can see the full extent of the damage, Cash. Both directions. There's…this… it's bad. It's so much worse than what it looks like on TV. I can smell gas and there are fires. So many people hurt. Gonna be some casualties. I figure other cities are mobilizing to send help, that whole Oklahoma Standard thing that happened after the Oklahoma City bombing, but Cash…" His voice cracked and he swallowed around the lump in his throat. "Cooper's in there with Britt and maybe his babies. We gotta get them out."

"We will, Bridge. That's a promise. We're working on this end. Cord is here. He's rounding up heavy equipment and crews. They'll be there as soon as they can. The roads…some are blocked. Near as we can tell, I-35 is still open. Do what you can until we get there."

Three black SUVs arrived. Cash, Cord and Chance were the first ones out, followed by employees from BarEx, Barron Security and Chance's law firm. A few minutes later, a semi-truck hauling a flatbed trailer pulled in. The oil field crews from BarEx abandoned what they'd been doing—shifting rubble by hand—to unload a front-end loader and bulldozer.

"Crane's stuck in traffic but will be here soon," the semi driver yelled over the noise. "Two pole trucks are on their way."

Over the next hour, more people and equipment arrived, along with a news crew from Channel 2. Bridger worked tirelessly. He wasn't surprised when Tucker, Deacon and Dillon arrived, not only ready to work but with messages from their brothers, Boone and Hunter, who were in Washington, DC, with their cousin, Senator Clay Barron. Kade Waite, the Barrons' half-brother, arrived with power tools from the Barron Ranch. Deacon's tour bus arrived, driven by Chase Barron. The Bee Dubyas were all onboard, along with Katherine Tate. The wives immediately set about distributing food and drink while Chase pulled on work gloves and asked where he was needed.

Bridger stopped dragging a chunk of concrete when

his mother touched his back. He straightened and almost refused the bottle of water she held out. He didn't want to stop. Stopping meant time to think, time to worry about his brother. Their last conversation about Britt hadn't been comfortable but he'd been worried about Cooper and wasn't sure about Britt. But hearing Cooper's voice? The worry in it? Cooper loved Britt and that was the bottom line. He loved his brother and he'd do whatever he could to help him win the woman he loved. All he had to do was rescue them alive and in one piece.

"Drink, son. You have to stay hydrated. You get sick, you can't help your brother or any of the others."

"They're in there, Mom." He just managed to keep his voice level.

"I know. And they'll be fine. Cooper always comes through a scrape unscathed."

"This isn't a scrape—"

"He's lucky, Bridger. And this isn't his first tornado. He's fine." She studied the path the rescue workers had carved toward the front entrance. "And probably sitting in there grousing about how long we're taking to get them out."

"I hope you're right, Mom."

She patted his arm. "I'm always right when it comes to you boys."

Britt's phone battery had died, along with those belonging to the medical personnel. Cooper was hoarding his remaining charge like a prepper facing Armageddon. The OR was basically intact, though the false ceiling had come down, bringing with it some of the medical equipment from the floor above. No injuries. Britt was resting, his daughter and son, both healthy, lay swaddled in blankets in her arms. He'd managed to get the door to the OR open and to shift some of the debris blocking the hallway, but there was no way to get Britt and the babies out. They'd just have to wait.

Cooper *knew* his family was outside doing their best to rescue him and the others. That's the way the Tates worked. And his Barron cousins would be there. At the moment, though, Britt and the babies consumed his thoughts. His attention focused on them as the nurse's voice ghosted through the darkness.

"What are their names?"

"Not sure," Britt murmured. "I'm thinking something literary."

"Oh? Like what?"

"Archie and Veronica."

He choked. She couldn't be serious. "No way—" The grumble of a diesel engine and the scrape of a metal blade on concrete cut off the rest of his protest.

Lights appeared and he snagged his cell phone, clicking on the flashlight app. "In here!" he yelled over the noise. The motor immediately cut off.

"Cooper?"

"We're in here, Bridger!"

"Are you okay?"

"We're good. All good."

His brother's head poked through the door. "Britt and the babies?"

"All good. I'm a dad," he said, his voice full of wonder. "A girl and a boy."

The message was passed back to the crowd outside and cheering ensued. Thirty minutes later, Britt and the twins were carried out in a Stokes basket as roughnecks, firefighters and a column of Tate and Barron brothers passed them over the debris. His mom, sisters-in-law and the Bee Dubyas clustered around the open doors of an ambulance.

Coop was torn. He should stay and help the rescuers get to the basement stairwell but the woman and babies he loved with all his heart were about to be shuttled off to another hospital. His mom gave him a quick hug.

"Get in the ambulance, son. There's plenty of help here. Your new family needs you more."

And they did.

Epilogue

Cooper glared at Britt. “We are not naming them after comic book characters.”

She offered up a cheeky grin. “We aren’t. *I* am.”

“Britt.”

“Cooper.”

The reverend looked from one to the other, her expression noncommittal though Coop caught the twitch of the woman’s lips. His entire family was gathered around the baptismal font of St. Paul’s Cathedral, the historic Episcopal Church in downtown Oklahoma City. Tucker and Zoe stood as godparents. He turned to his brother for backup.

Tucker raised his hands. “I’m not getting in the middle of this.”

Zoe laughed. "Me neither. I'm the last one to throw stones about baby names."

Cooper snapped his mouth shut. This was true. She'd named her son Nashville Vanderbilt Parker, which was then legally changed to Nash Parker Tate when Tucker formally adopted the little boy.

The reverend cleared her throat. "Can we proceed?" She continued with the ceremony after Cooper huffed out an aggrieved sigh. When she reached the part in the baptismal sacrament when she announced the babies' names, Cooper sucked in a breath.

"Daniella Katherine Tate and Denver Owens Tate."

"Daniella Katherine for my dad and your mom and Denver Owens for your dad and my family name." Britt's eyes glistened with tears.

Cooper bent and kissed them off her cheeks. "I love you, Girl Wonder."

"Good, because I love you too."

He opened his mouth, then closed it. He didn't want to fight. Not today of all days. Then the woman he adored beyond all reason surprised him.

"Aren't you going to ask?"

"Ask what?"

"Huh. Seriously?"

Then it dawned on him. Except he wouldn't ask her again.

She arched a brow, looking imperious. "You'll never know if you don't ask."

"I've already asked."

"So. Ask again."

"Fine. Marry me."

“That’s not a question.”

“Okay. Will you—”

“Down on one knee, Hero Boy.”

He glanced around. His entire family grinned at him. He dropped to one knee, but Tucker tapped him on the shoulder before he could continue.

“You’re gonna need this, big brother.”

Bridger, having stopped by Cooper’s house, placed the ring box Cooper had hidden in his sock drawer all these months in his hand. He popped the lid and in a voice that sounded a tad hesitant, he asked, “Britt Owens, will you marry me?”

“Yes.”

He managed to scramble to his feet and jam the ring on her finger before she changed her mind. His family cheered. The woman he loved had agreed—finally—to be his wife and their baby daughter and son were healthy and very much loved. Cooper Tate truly was comfortable in his own skin, and in his new, and wonderful life.

* * * * *

COMING NEXT MONTH FROM

Available March 9, 2021

#2791 AT THE RANCHER'S PLEASURE

Texas Cattleman's Club: Heir Apparent • by Joss Wood

Runaway groom Brett Harston was Royal's favorite topic until Sarabeth Edmonds returned. Banished years before by her ex-husband, she's determined to reclaim her life and reputation. But a spontaneous kiss meant to rile up town gossips unleashes a passionate romance neither can ignore...

#2792 CRAVING A REAL TEXAN

The Texas Tremaines • by Charlene Sands

Grieving CEO Cade Tremaine retreats to his family's cabin and finds gorgeous chef Harper Dawn. She's wary and hiding her identity after rejecting a televised proposal, but their spark is immediate. Will the Texan find a second chance at love, or will Harper's secret drive him away?

#2793 WAKING UP MARRIED

The Bourbon Brothers • by Reese Ryan

One passionate Vegas night finds bourbon executive Zora Abbott married to her friend Dallas Hamilton. To protect their reputations after their tipsy vows go viral, they agree to stay married for one year. But their fake marriage is realer and hotter than they could've imagined!

#2794 HOW TO LIVE WITH TEMPTATION

by Fiona Brand

Billionaire Tobias Hunt has always believed the beautiful Allegra Mallory was only after his money. Now, forced to live and work together, she claims a fake fiancé to prove she isn't interested. But with sparks flying, Tobias wants what he can no longer have...

#2795 AFTER HOURS ATTRACTION

404 Sound • by Kianna Alexander

After finding out his ex embezzled funds, recording COO Gage Woodson has sworn off workplace romance. But when he's stranded with his assistant, Ainsley Voss, on a business trip, their chemistry is too hot to ignore. Will they risk their working relationship for something more?

#2796 HIS PERFECT FAKE ENGAGEMENT

Men of Maddox Hill • by Shannon McKenna

When a scandal jeopardizes playboy CEO Drew Maddox's career, he proposes a fake engagement to his brilliant and philanthropic friend Jenna Sommers to revitalize his reputation and fund her efforts. But as passion takes over, can this bad boy reform his ways for her?

YOU CAN FIND MORE INFORMATION ON UPCOMING HARLEQUIN TITLES, FREE EXCERPTS AND MORE AT HARLEQUIN.COM.

HDCNM0221

SPECIAL EXCERPT FROM

HARLEQUIN

DESIRE

When a scandal jeopardizes playboy CEO Drew Maddox's career, he proposes a fake engagement to his brilliant and philanthropic friend Jenna Sommers to revitalize his reputation and fund her efforts. But as passion takes over, can this bad boy reform his ways for her?

Read on for a sneak peek at
His Perfect Fake Engagement
by New York Times *bestselling author Shannon McKenna!*

Drew pulled her toward the big Mercedes SUV idling at the curb. "Here's your ride," he said. "We still on for tonight? I wouldn't blame you if you changed your mind. The paparazzi are a huge pain in the ass. Like a weather condition. Or a zombie horde."

"I'm still game," she said. "Let `em do their worst."

That got her a smile that touched off fireworks at every level of her consciousness.

For God's sake. Get a grip, girl.

"I'll pick you up for dinner at eight fifteen," he said. "Our reservation at Peccati di Gola is at eight forty-five."

"I'll be ready," she promised.

"Can I put my number into your phone, so you can text me your address?"

"Of course." She handed him her phone and waited as he tapped the number into it. He hit Call and waited for the ring.

"There," she said, taking her phone back. "You've got me now."

"Lucky me," he murmured. He glanced back at the photographers, still blocked by three security men at the door, still snapping photos. "You're no delicate flower, are you?"

"By no means," she assured him.

"I like that," he said. He'd already opened the car door for her, but as she was about to get inside, he pulled her swiftly back up again and covered her mouth with his.

His kiss was hotter than the last one. Deliberate, demanding. He pressed her closer, tasting her lips.

Oh. Wow. He tasted amazing. Like fire, like wind. Like sunlight on the ocean. She dug her fingers into the massive bulk of his shoulders, or tried to. He was so thick and solid. Her fingers slid helplessly over the fabric of his jacket. They could get no grip.

His lips parted hers. The tip of his tongue flicked against hers, coaxed her to open, to give herself up. To yield to him. His kiss promised infinite pleasure in return. It demanded surrender on a level so deep and primal, she responded instinctively.

She melted against him with a shudder of emotion that was absolutely unfaked.

Holy crap. Panic pierced her as she realized what was happening. He'd kissed her like he meant it, and she'd responded in the same way. As naturally as breathing.

She was so screwed.

Jenna pulled away, shaking. She felt like a mask had been pulled off. That he could see straight into the depths of her most private self.

And Drew helped her into the car and gave her a reassuring smile and a friendly wave as the car pulled away, like it was no big deal. As if he hadn't just tongue-kissed her passionately in front of a crowd of photographers and caused an inner earthquake.

Her lips were still glowing. They tingled from the contact.

She couldn't let her mind stray down this path. She was a means to an end.

It was Drew Maddox's nature to be seductive. He was probably that way with every woman he talked to. He probably couldn't help himself. Not even if he tried.

She had to keep that fact firmly in mind.

All. The. Time.

HDEXP0221